Shantytown

Shantytown

•

CÉSAR AIRA

Translated by Chris Andrews

A NEW DIRECTIONS PAPERBOOK ORIGINAL

Manufactured in the United States of America
New Directions Books are printed on acid-free paper
First published as a New Directions Paperbook Original (NDP1268) in 2013
Design by Erik Rieselbach

Library of Congress Cataloging-in-Publication Data
Aira, César, 1949–
[Villa. English]
Shantytown / César Aira ; Translated from the Spanish by Chris Andrews.
pages cm
"A New Directions Paperbook Original."
ISBN 978-0-8112-1911-2 (alk. paper)
I. Andrews, Chris, 1962–, translator. II. Title.
PQ7798.1.I7V5513 2013
863'.64—dc23   2013027464

10 9 8 7 6 5 4 3

New Directions Books are published for James Laughlin
by New Directions Publishing Corporation
80 Eighth Avenue, NY 10011

SHANTYTOWN

I

ONE WAY MAXI CHOSE TO SPEND HIS TIME WAS HELPING the local cardboard collectors to transport their loads. An act performed once, on the spur of the moment, had developed over time into a job that he took very seriously. It had begun with something as natural as relieving a child or a pregnant woman of a load that seemed too great for someone like that to bear (although the woman or the child was, in fact, bearing it). Before long he was indiscriminately helping children and adults, men and women: he was bigger and stronger than any of them, and anyway he did it because he wanted to, not because he was asked. It never occurred to him to see it as an act of charity or solidarity or Christian duty or pity or anything like that. It was something he did, that was all. It was spontaneous, like a hobby. Had anybody asked him why, he would have had trouble explaining, given how terribly hard it was for Maxi to express himself, and in his own mind he didn't even try to justify what he was doing. As time went by, his dedication to the task increased, and if one day, or rather one night, he had been unable to do his rounds in the neighborhood, he would have had the uncomfortable feeling that the collectors were missing him and thinking, "Where can he be? Why hasn't he come? Is he angry with us?" But he never missed a night. There were no other obligations to keep him from going out at that time.

The expression *cardboard collectors* was a euphemism, which everyone had adopted, and it conveyed the intended meaning clearly enough (although the less delicate *scavengers* served that purpose too). Cardboard, or paper, was only one of their specialties. They also collected glass, cans, wood ... in fact, where there is need, there is no specialization. They had to find a way to get by and they weren't going to turn up their noses, not even at the remnants of food that they found in the garbage bags. And perhaps those borderline or spoiled leftovers were, in fact, the real objective, and all the rest — cardboard, glass, wood, tin — no more than a respectable front.

In any case, Maxi didn't ask himself why they were doing what they did. He tactfully averted his gaze when he saw them rummaging through the trash, as if all that mattered to him were the loads that they assembled, and only their weight, not their contents. He didn't even ask himself why he was doing what *he* did. He did it because he could, because he felt like it, because it gave his evening walk a purpose. When he began, in autumn, he would set off in the sinister half-light of dusk, but by the time the habit was entrenched, the year had turned, and it was dark when he started. That was when the collectors came out, not because they wanted to, or were trying to work under cover of night, but because people put out their trash at the end of the day, and, as soon as they did, the race was on to beat the garbage trucks, which came and took it all away.

That time of day had always been hard for Maxi ever since he was a boy, and now that he was entering his twenties, it was even worse. He suffered from so-called "night blindness," which of course is not blindness at all, just a troublesome incapacity to distinguish things in dim or artificial light. As a result of this problem (or was it the cause?) his circadian rhythm was markedly diurnal. He woke up at first light, without fail, and the shutdown of all his systems at nightfall was sudden and irrevocable. As a child he had fitted in well, because that's the natural rhythm of children, but in his teenage years he had started to lose touch with his friends and classmates. They were all eagerly exploring the night, enjoying the freedom it granted them, coming to maturity as they learned its lessons. He had tried too, without success, and had given up some time ago. His path was solitary, all his own. At the age of about fifteen, already falling out of step with the routines and pursuits of his peers, he had started going to the gym. His body responded very well to weight training, and he had developed muscles everywhere. He was very tall and solidly built; without the training he would have been fat. As it was, when people saw him in the street, they thought: "meathead" or "brainless hulk," and they weren't too far from the truth.

In March he had sat exams for some of the subjects that he still had to pass to get his high school diploma, and there would be more in July or December ... or not. His studies had languished in a slow but steady and definitive way. Looking to the future, both he and his parents had come to accept that he'd never go back to being a student: he wasn't cut out for it; there was no point. This was confirmed by looking back: he'd forgotten almost everything that he'd learned in the long years spent at high school. At the intersection of the future and the past were those aptly named *preliminary* subjects, suspended in a truly perplexing uncertainty. So when that autumn began, he was at a loose end. Over the summer he'd studied in a desultory sort of way, and his parents were resigned to the fact that he always took a long break after exams, not to recover from the effort so much as from the sad, inadequate feeling that came over him when he studied. Although he had flunked the three exams in March, or maybe because of that, the gulf between him and the world of education deepened even further. In theory he was supposed to try again in July, and then, according to the plan, re-sit exams for another two subjects (or was it three?), but he couldn't even think about studying, and nobody reminded him. So his only activity was going to the gym. His father, a wealthy businessman, didn't pressure him to look for work. There would be time for him to find his way. He was a biddable, affectionate young man, happy to stay at home; quite the opposite of his only sibling, a younger sister, who was rebellious and headstrong. They lived in a comfortable modern apartment near Plaza Flores.

There were a number of reasons why Maxi had begun to go walking in the evenings at the end of summer. One was that, around that time, the arguments between his mother and his sister tended to intensify and fill the apartment with shouting. Another was that his body, by then, had energy to spend, and a sort of alarm had begun to sound. He went to the gym in the morning, from opening time until midday. After lunch he took a nap, and after that he watched television, did some shopping, hung around at home.... During those long hours of inactivity he grew increasingly restless, and in the end he simply had to get himself moving again. He had tried running in Parque Chacabuco, but his body was a bit too heavy, too muscular, and his gym instructor had advised him against it, because the jolting could upset the delicate balance of his joints, which were already under stress from the weight of muscle. Anyway, he didn't enjoy it. Walking, on the other hand, was the ideal form of exercise. His walks coincided with the appearance of the collectors, and that coincidence was how it all began.

Cardboard collecting or scavenging had gradually established itself as an occupation over the previous ten or fifteen years. It was no longer a novelty. The collectors had become invisible because they operated discreetly, almost furtively, at night (and only for a while), but above all because they took refuge in a social recess that most people prefer to ignore.

They came from the crowded shantytowns in Lower Flores, to which they returned with their booty. Some worked all alone (in which case Maxi left them to it), or driving a horse and cart. But most of them worked in family groups and pulled their carts themselves. If Maxi had stopped to wonder whether or not they'd accept his help, or tried to find the right words, it would never have happened. But one day he came across a child or a pregnant woman (he couldn't remember which), barely able to shift an enormous bag, and he took it from the child's or woman's hands, just like that, without a word, lifted it up as if it were a feather and carried it to the corner, where the cart was. That first time, perhaps, they said thank you, and went away thinking,

"What a nice boy." He had broken the ice. Before long he could help anyone, even the men: they didn't take offence; they pointed out where they'd left their carts, and off he went. Nothing was heavy for him; he could have carried the collectors as well, under the other arm. They were tough, resilient people, but scrawny and malnourished, worn out by their trudging, and very light. The only precaution he learned to take was to look into the cart before loading it up, because there was often a baby on board. From the age of two, the children scampered around among the piles of garbage bags with their mothers, helping, in their way, with the search, learning the trade. If the family was in a hurry and the children were lagging behind, rather than listening to the impatient shouting of the parents, Maxi would pick up all the kids, as if gathering toys to tidy a room, and head for the cart. Actually, they were always in a hurry because they were racing against the garbage trucks, which were hard on their heels in certain streets. And ahead of them, in the next block, they could see big piles of promising bags (they had an intuitive sense of where it would be worth their while to stop), and this made them anxious: an urgent buzz would spread through the group; some would shoot off ahead, the father and one of the sons, for example, because the father was the best at undoing the knots and opening the bags and spotting the good stuff in the dark; meanwhile the mother would stay behind pulling the cart, because they couldn't leave it too far away.... That's where Maxi came in. He'd tell her to join her husband; he'd bring the vehicle. That was something he could do; all the rest was up to them. He'd grip the two handles, and whether the cart was empty or full (sometimes it was piled high), he'd pull it along almost effortlessly, as if he were playing a game, using his excess strength to stop it jolting, so as to spare the mended axle and the dicey wheels, and not to disturb the baby asleep inside.

All the local scavengers got to know him eventually, though he couldn't tell them apart, not that it mattered to him. Some would wait for him, watching a corner, and when they saw him coming, they'd rush to get ready: he saved them time, that was the main thing. They didn't say much, hardly a word, not even the children, who are usually so talkative. He'd come across a group of them almost as soon as he stepped into the street, but sometimes he'd go across to the other side of Rivadavia and the railway line, where they congregated earlier in the evening, and then he'd accompany their slow southward march, passing from one family to another. When they stopped to work a specially rich vein, and he left them behind, they never tried to stop him; it was as if they realized that others, a little further on, needed him more than they did.

If there was some sharing of the places with the richest pick-ings, it was a customary, tacit arrangement, or perhaps a matter of instinct. Maxi never saw them fight, or even get in each other's way. When two groups met at a corner, he was the only link be-tween them. His imposing presence must have been enough to establish order and guarantee peace: for these diminutive, down-trodden people, his giant's body served as a bond of solidarity.

Marching southward, they were heading for home, that is, for the shantytown; as their loads grew heavier, the distance to be covered shrank. But they were also preceding the garbage trucks, which advanced in the same direction. This was such a practical arrangement, it might have been set up deliberately.

The richest plunder was to be found near Avenida Rivadavia, in the cross streets and the parallel streets, packed with tall apartment buildings, restaurants, greengrocers, and other stores. If the collectors couldn't find what they were after in that stretch, they wouldn't find it anywhere. When they got to Directorio, if things had gone well, they could relax and rummage in a more leisurely way through the less numerous piles of trash. There was always something unexpected: a little piece of furniture, a mattress, a gadget or an ornament, and curious objects whose purpose could not be guessed simply by looking at them. If there was room, they put these spoils into the cart; if not, they tied them on with ropes brought specially for that purpose. It looked as if they were moving house: the volume of what they ended up hauling must have been equivalent to that of all their worldly goods, yet it was the fruit of a single day's work; when all the deals were done, it would be worth a few coins. By this stage, the women had generally identified anything edible and put it into the plastic bags that they were carrying. Beyond Directorio they entered the housing projects: a dark, deserted tangle of crescent streets lined with little houses. The pickings were much slimmer there, but that didn't matter. The collectors hurried on, anxious now to get back as soon as possible. They took short cuts down the little alleys to Bonorino, which led to the shantytown. But they were tired and burdened; the children stumbled along half asleep, and the carts wandered erratically. Marching home, they looked like refugees fleeing from a war zone.

By this time of night, Maxi had to struggle to keep his eyes open. Dinnertime was late at his place, luckily, but he got up early and needed lots of sleep. As he was helping his last family, if he was sure that they really were the last, he'd be waiting for the moment when he could say goodbye and go home, which he usually did when they came out onto Calle Bonorino. From there on they continued straight ahead, and he went back in the opposite direction (he lived on the corner of Bonorino and Bonifacio). The collectors, however, often made detours, which took them beyond the projects, into ill-defined areas occupied by factories, warehouses, and vacant lots. And there it was sometimes the other way around: they said goodbye to him, because, on the spur of the moment, or in accordance with a pre-established plan (Maxi couldn't tell: his rudimentary conversations with them never got that far), they would stop in some derelict building or open space that could serve as a refuge. This surprised him, and he could never work out why they did it. Obviously they were tired, but not so tired they couldn't make it home. Perhaps it was so they wouldn't have to share the food that they were carrying with relatives or neighbors. Perhaps they had nowhere to live, or just a portion of some flimsy little shack, and it was more comfortable for them to set up a provisional camp. One advantage of going out to work all together, as a family, was that wherever they happened to stop instantly became their home.

In any case, as long as the family kept moving, Maxi put off the moment of saying goodbye. As long as he wasn't asleep on his feet, he could do a bit more to help them. He didn't like having to leave them to their fate, they looked so exhausted; and it was no trouble, he enjoyed it. They trusted him, and his strength was plain for all to see. Imagine an elephant pulling a baby carriage: that's how easy it was. Soon all the collectors got to know him. They accepted his help without fuss and gratefully let him take the handles of their carts, even those who looked unfamiliar to him, either because they were new to the trade, or came from another neighborhood, or hadn't yet happened to cross his path (or because he was getting them mixed up, since he had no memory for faces, and there were so many of them, and they looked so alike, not to mention his poor night vision). And perhaps they didn't need to have seen him to know who he was, because the news of his existence had spread among them like a legend: a humble, realist legend, so they weren't amazed when it became a reality.

For the last part of the way, if there was room, he lifted the children up onto the cart, and as he pulled it along he could feel them falling asleep. If there was room, with a smile and a gesture, he would invite the mother to climb up as well. She would smile timidly, as if for the first time in her life, and ask, "Are you sure it won't be too heavy?" This was just good manners, because he could obviously manage, but he would hasten to reply that it was no trouble at all. "Please! Up you go, all of you!" And he'd look at the father as if to say, "Make the most of it." If the little man climbed up too, the whole family would roll along, riding the rickshaw, seated on their trove of trash. Sometimes an older boy would refuse to get up, out of pride, or because he thought it would be "too much," but there was nothing contemptuous or aggressive about this refusal: on the contrary, the boy identified with the good giant who was towing the rest of his family, and watched him out of the corner of his eye, feeling proud, admiring his voluminous muscles bulging in the moonlight. More than once, at times like that, as he pulled a whole family along, Maxi felt that he had actually fallen asleep on his feet.

From the intersection with Rivadavia, where Calle Bonorino began, all the signs said "Avenida Esteban Bonorino," but no one knew why, because it was a narrow street like any other. Just another bureaucratic error, it was generally assumed, made by some careless civil servant who had ordered the painting of the signs without ever having set foot in the neighborhood. But the name was actually correct, although in such a secret way that no one realized. Eighteen blocks from Rivadavia, further than anyone would choose to walk, beyond numerous high-rise apartment buildings and warehouses and sheds and vacant lots, just when Calle Bonorino seemed to be petering out, it widened to become the avenue that the signs had been promising from the start. But this wasn't the beginning; it was the end. The avenue continued for barely a hundred yards, leading only to a long sealed road that ran off along the edge of the shantytown. Maxi had never gone that far, but he'd gone far enough to see: in contrast with the dark stretch of road leading up to it, the shantytown was strangely illuminated, almost radiant, crowned with a halo that shone in the fog. It was almost like seeing a vision, in the distance, and this fantastic impression was intensified by his "night blindness" and the sleepiness besetting him already. Seen like that, at night and far away, the shantytown might have seemed a magical place, but he was not entirely naïve; he knew that its inhabitants lived in squalor and desperation. Perhaps it was shame that prompted the scavengers to say goodbye to him before they reached their destination. Perhaps they wanted this handsome, well-dressed young man, whose curious pastime it was to assist them, to believe that they lived in a distant and mysterious place, rather than going into the depressing details. But although they can't have failed to notice Maxi's purity—which shone in his beautiful childlike face, his clear eyes, his perfect teeth, his cropped hair, and his clothes, which were always freshly washed and ironed—they were hardly in a position to exercise that kind of tact.

Another thing that they must have noticed was the sleepiness that overwhelmed him toward the end: it was massive and irresistible. They might have been worried that he would actually fall asleep: what would they do with him then? It was an infantile characteristic: he was a child in the overdeveloped body of an athlete, whose energy was spent in weight training instead of play, and in voluntarily hauling loads of trash. Then there was his very marked diurnal rhythm, determined by a chemical imbalance in his hypothalamus, which affected his pupils (thence his "night blindness"). And as if that were not enough (but all these factors were interrelated), he always got up very early. Earlier than he should have, in fact, because of something that happened by chance. Well before eight, when the gym opened, he was up and dressed and had eaten his breakfast. In summer, when it was light at five, and he didn't feel like just waiting around, he had got into the habit of packing his bag, leaving an hour early, and filling in the time with a walk. On those walks he had noticed a boy who clearly had no home or family and was sleeping under the freeway. The place was strange: one of those gaps that the freeway had created when it cut a brutal swathe through the city, a triangular area bounded on two sides by streets, which the council had turned into a little gravel park. They had put in cement benches and flower beds, but it wasn't the right place for a park, and it fell into neglect straight away. It was completely overgrown with tall grass and weeds, except for a narrow path which people in the neighborhood must have used to go from one street to the other, cutting the corner. The freeway loomed over it like an enormous curved cornice. One day Maxi happened to pass by first thing in the morning and saw the boy sitting against the wall, putting on his sneakers. As he walked past, the boy watched him warily, and Maxi realized that he had spent the night there, sheltered by the freeway and the place's dereliction. Among the weeds, Maxi glimpsed some newspapers, which the boy must have been using as a bed, and a bag, which must have contained his possessions. A few days later he went past again, at the same time, and again the boy was about to leave. That abandoned space was his bedroom, apparently: nobody passed that way at night, and he left at the break of day. Only Maxi had seen him there. The first few times, the boy seemed to resent the intrusion, but after that he let Maxi go by without even looking up. Maxi got the feeling that the boy didn't mind him walking past each day, now that his secret had been discovered: it could become a part of his routine, and even provide a kind of company—although they didn't speak to each other—a make-shift substitute for the family and friends he didn't have. Perhaps when the boy saw him go past, he thought, "There he is again, my anonymous friend," or something like that. You never know what people will fasten onto, when they're all alone and they have nothing else. And that boy had as little as it was possible to have. Maxi called him "the hobo." What he did during the day, how he fed himself and how he spent his time were mysteries; he must have stayed fairly close by so that he could come back and sleep in the same place every night. A few steps away, toward the edge of the little triangle, was a place where the weeds were higher and thicker, and it gave off a nasty smell; that must have been where the hobo did his business. It was hard to tell his age, but he didn't have a beard, so he couldn't have been more than sixteen or seventeen. He was thin and small, with jet black hair, pale skin, sunken eyes, and the face of a frightened animal. He wore a kind of blue suit, which was dirty and crumpled.

Maxi wasn't absolutely sure that the hobo actually slept there; he'd always seen him up and dressed, except for that first time when he was putting on his sneakers. But that didn't prove anything: people often take their shoes off to remove stones and things; then they have to put them back on again. Also, memory had transformed that first time into something strange and uncertain, as it often does when a situation is repeated over and again. There were other clues of course, like the newspapers laid on the ground, the bad smell, and most importantly, the fact that the hobo was there without fail every morning. But that in itself was perplexing. The timing of Maxi's morning walks was irregular, and yet the boy was always at the same point in his routine: awake already but not yet gone. It might just have been a coincidence, but still it was strange. Maxi started setting out earlier, to see if he could catch him sleeping. But he never did. The only explanation was that the hobo got up at cockcrow, with the very first light of day. But why was he always standing on his newspapers, as if he had just woken up? Was he waiting for Maxi? Was he using him as a sign that it was time to leave? Maxi might have tested this hypothesis by going past later in the morning, to see if the hobo really would wait, but he preferred to pursue the opposite strategy of passing earlier each day, in the hope of finding him sound asleep. And that was why he got up so early, bolted his breakfast and left; and then in the evening he had to pay the price: as soon as it got dark he could barely stay awake.

II

AS WINTER CAME ON, NIGHT FELL SLIGHTLY EARLIER with every passing day, and the scavengers stopped a little sooner, and Maxi went a few steps further toward the shantytown before turning back. Since the garbage trucks kept doing their rounds at the same time, there was really no reason for this acceleration, unless the collectors were rushing through their work because of the cold, eager to get back to their shelters, or maybe people were bringing out their trash earlier, reacting automatically to the failing of the light. It was also possible that Maxi's help was making a difference. His action was individual, spontaneous and technically primitive, but perhaps it was having an overall effect and lightening the burden for all the collectors. If so, it was inexplicable and could only be attributed to the mystery of charity. In any case, they were now reaching Directorio by eight (whereas in summer it had taken till nine), and as Maxi approached the place where Bonorino opened out, he was less sleepy and had more energy in reserve. It also helped that he wasn't getting up so early, because the sun was rising later. These advantages were counterbalanced by an accentuation of his diurnal rhythm, and a heavier, thicker sleepiness; the body consumes more energy in cold weather, and he was an eminently physical being.

No matter what the load, Maxi hauled without effort, like a faithful workhorse never shrinking from the yoke, and each day he ventured one step further into sleep.... No one had made any effort to discover Maxi's social function, but he had found it on his own, without looking, guided by chance and the need to occupy his time. The reason why he had been left to his own devices was simple: society works with classes far too broad and crude to capture the variable properties of an individual. No one was to blame, of course. How can you tell what a person is capable of doing? There is no science of vocations. Each person's place is determined by chance, and inadaptation is the norm. If there were a procedure for deciding what people should do by taking every one of their qualities into account, it would determine their maximum utility, both to those around them and to society in general. For a young man like Maxi, disinclined to study and endowed with an impressive (and, in its way, decorative) physique, the obvious occupation would have been to work as a bouncer or a security guard at a nightclub. He could have walked into a job like that; they were hiring just about anyone—the demand was insatiable. But here we can begin to see how this kind of selection and placement is based on generalizations. Maxi's particularities rendered him unsuitable: for a start, his "night blindness" ruled out working at night. And then he didn't have the gift of violence. So the only remaining option, in the system of general categories, was to work as a gym instructor. But that possibility was ruled out too, by less obvious particularities. He couldn't accept or even consider a job like that. To him, there was something monstrous about the idea of someone who worked out in a gym becoming an instructor: it was like a patient becoming a doctor. He had a deep and instinctive aversion to systems that fed into themselves (he wouldn't have been able to say why). It was as if, in order to exist at all, his strength and, in a sense, his beauty, had to operate outside the structure that had produced them, engaging with the real world. His "work" with the families of collectors was an improvised, spontaneous solution, which he adopted without a second thought, as if it were a gift from heaven. He had no doubt that in time he would find his real work, his vocation. And perhaps this was not just a stopgap measure, to fill in the time, but a path.

Every new cart he pulled was different. But in spite of this variety, all of them were suited to the common purpose of transporting loads as quickly and easily as possible. Carts like that could not be bought, or found in the junk that people threw away. The collectors built them, probably from junk, but the bits and pieces that went into them came from all sorts of things, some of which were nothing like a cart. Maxi was hardly one to consider things from an aesthetic point of view, least of all these carts; but as it happened he was able to appreciate them more intimately than any observer because he was using them. More than that: he was yoked to them. He had noticed how they were all different, in height, capacity, length, width, depth, wheel size ... in every way, really. Some were made with planks, sticks, or pipes, others with wire mesh or canvas or even cardboard. The wheels were from a great variety of vehicles: bicycles, motorcycles, tricycles, baby carriages, even cars. Naturally, no two carts looked the same, and each had its own particular beauty, its value as folk art. This was not an entirely new phenomenon. The historians of Buenos Aires had traced the evolution of the city's carts and their decoration: the ingenious inscriptions and decorative painting (the renowned *fileteado*). But now it was different. This was the nineteen nineties and things had changed. These carts didn't have inscriptions or painting or anything like that. They were purely functional, and since they were built from assembled odds and ends, their beauty was, in a sense, automatic or objective, and therefore very modern, too modern for any historian to bother with.

As Maxi's hauling brought him each night a little closer, the light the shantytown gave off gradually came into focus. One night he finally reached the point where Calle Bonorino opened out. That was when he realized that it really was an avenue, like the signs said.... But only there, and that was where it ended: on one side there was a row of little houses and stores; on the other, some kind of warehouse with a yard. In fact, the avenue was so wide and so short, it was more like a big square parking lot. On the far side, a sealed road led off into the distance, gently curving away. To one side of this road lay the shantytown, shining like a gem lit up from within. The strangeness of this spectacle brought him to a halt. The father and the mother (who had been riding on the cart) climbed down and took hold of the handles, supposing that his assistance had, for that night, come to an end. He yielded submissively, took his leave with a shy smile, and set off homeward. Before re-entering the narrow part of Bonorino, he turned to look back: the cart's receding silhouette stood out against the brightness. He was very sleepy and had a long walk ahead of him, and yet somehow he was reluctant to go home. It may have been a purely physiological reflex; perhaps his dysfunctional pupils were attracted to that excess of light.

It might seem odd that a shantytown should be so abundantly lit. But there was a perfectly reasonable explanation. The connection to the grid was illegal; everyone knew that the shanty-dwellers "pirated" electricity. Since they weren't paying, they could use it as lavishly as they liked. It's easy enough to run a line from a high tension cable, but someone has to do it, someone who knows how to make the connections and distribute the current. There were, as it turned out, plenty of electricians in the shantytown, as there were plenty of people skilled in all the other trades, to a basic level at least. You could almost have said that everyone there had all-round basic skills: poor people learn to make do; they have no choice. They didn't fear electricity like middle-class people, and there was no good reason why they should. But there was something odd: whenever Maxi managed to get a brief glimpse into the shacks, through open doors or windows, those spaces were much more modestly illuminated. In contrast with the blaze outside, the interiors were dim.

Up until then he'd thought that the scavengers were ashamed to let him come right up to their dwellings; but now he began to think that they'd been acting out of kindness: noticing how sleepy he was, they had been letting him go. He resolved to be more alert and extended his siestas; in vain, because nightfall still had the same effect on him. Nevertheless, by hiding his tiredness, he was able to get closer, and finally, one momentous night, he finally crossed the shantytown's perimeter, and ventured just a few steps into that enchanted kingdom of unstinting light.

The streets were very narrow, barely the width of a car, and the few ancient, rusty cars there were, often stripped of wheels or windows or doors, completely blocked the way. The strangest thing was the layout of the streets: they weren't perpendicular to the edge of the shantytown, but ran off at an angle of about 45 degrees. Their relative straightness was also strange, given the haphazard way in which the shacks had been built. The edge of the shantytown curved away gradually, suggesting that its over-all shape was an enormous circle. It was densely populated. How many people would have been living there? Tens of thousands. The streets were more or less evenly spaced, and all ran off at the same angle. And it was via one or other of those streets that Maxi went in, that first night and the nights that followed, depending on the address of the people he happened to be helping, who were different every time.

The overall brightness resulted from the number of light bulbs suspended in the streets. Since the electricity was free, why skimp? They were ordinary 100-watt bulbs, hanging from cables tangled in the air. It looked festive: a garland of ten little bulbs, a bunch of half a dozen, a circle of fifteen or twenty, or rows—single, double, triple—or just two bulbs and a third above them, making a triangle.... Every kind of combination, all jumbled up, in a display of fanciful creativity. It was like a natural growth, as if at this level of society—the lowest—technology had been reab-sorbed by nature. As the days went by, Maxi began to realize that the number and arrangement of the bulbs was never the same from street to street: each had its own pattern of lights, which must have functioned like a name. It would have been easier to number them, but if the shantytown really was circular, as Maxi thought, numbering the streets would have been no use, because a circle has no beginning or end.

Every time he went down one of those oblique alleys, under the bunches of light bulbs, he was filled with a feeling of wonder. He felt privileged, but he didn't know why. It was no privilege to enter that malodorous labyrinth of tin shacks, where the poorest of the poor huddled for shelter. But that was just it: he wasn't poor, so if they invited him in, it was proof that they trusted him. He would have been willing to bet that no one he knew from school or the gym or his neighborhood and none of his family friends had ever set foot in a shantytown, or ever would. And yet they lived so close to one! It was just around the corner, really. So maybe it wasn't a big deal, except that, in a way, it was. Outsiders never went there, for a number of reasons, which all came down to one thing: fear. It's true that there was no real reason why outsiders would want to go there in the first place. But that was a part of the fear. And fear is the key to all places: social, geographical, even imaginary. It is the matrix of places, bringing them into existence and making it possible to move from one to another. Being or not being in a place depends on a complex system of actions, and it is well known that action engenders and nourishes fear. And besides, there must have been something to it: he'd heard that not even the police dared to go into the shantytowns.

Maxi's feeling of wonder completely overturned an earlier belief. He had assumed that the inhabitants of the shantytown had initially kept him out because they were ashamed, and finally allowed him in when they had come to trust him and felt that they no longer had anything to hide. But that reasoning rested on assumptions about familiarization, communication, the growth of trust, or some psychological process of that kind, and any such process would have required a constant subject: that is, it could only have occurred if he had been helping the same collectors every time. But in fact they were always different.

No. It must have been something else. He began to think it might be just the opposite. It wasn't shame or embarrassment, as he had stupidly supposed, projecting his middle-class values— why would they be ashamed of their homes, when he'd seen them rummaging through trash, looking for things to eat?—it was the other way around: they hadn't considered him worthy, because of what he was: a rich kid with fancy clothes. And it was only by hauling carts for months and making himself useful in a thousand different ways, putting his strength and kindness at their disposal, that he had earned the right to set foot in their domain. This was like a revelation for him, and it made him see things from a different point of view.

For a start, although he wasn't at all observant, he noticed that all the streets (if you could call those alleyways "streets") led inward and were never intersected by others running crossways. When one street intersects with another, it means there's a network, which seems natural: that's the way cities have always developed. But perhaps it isn't necessary; perhaps it's just a convention. This destitute city within the city might have been subject to laws of its own. But the layout did seem to be rather wasteful, considering how fiercely space was saved in every other way. The overcrowding was incredible; the shacks were absurdly small and crammed together, for reasons that apparently applied to shantytowns everywhere: these settlements sprang up in strictly limited spaces, and the population was continually growing because of unplanned reproduction as well as migration from the inland provinces and neighboring countries. So great, indeed, was the pressure for space that the mere existence of streets, narrow as they were, might have seemed surprising. But rational city planning saves space by multiplying streets, not by getting rid of them. The proof of that was close at hand, in the projects with their little houses, which the collectors had to pass through on their way back to the shantytown. The streets there were only thirty yards apart, which meant that each house was on a plot of land fifteen yards deep. In a conventional grid where the streets are a hundred yards apart, there are large unused areas at the backs of the properties. In the shantytown, the streets were forty or fifty yards apart, and if the shacks that fronted onto them had a maximum depth of five yards, as it was reasonable to suppose (their size was limited by the scarcity of materials), what occupied the space between the back of one shack and the back of the corresponding shack in the next street? The answer could only be: more shacks. There must have been even poorer families living back there, who reached their dwellings via narrow passageways between the shacks with street frontage.

Anyone in the habit of walking around in cities will have wondered, at some point, what there might be in the space behind the houses; and the rare opportunities to find out (by looking out from the back of a tall building, or down a long hallway when, for some reason, a door has been left open) are never disappointing. On the contrary, discovering that our fantasies have fallen short of reality, we are spurred on to imagine spaces that are even stranger and more exotic, more hidden, more mysterious. There are manicured and overgrown gardens, woods that have sprung up unbidden, fountains, statues, swimming pools, or huge constructions, sheds built for indeterminate purposes, workshops, the follies of hobbyists: miniature reproductions of castles or cathedrals, complete with scaled-down details, lovingly crafted and accumulated over the years, tricking the eye, distorting the overall perspective, which cannot be corrected from within the block for want of reliable reference points. All such fantasies were out of place in the shantytown. But precisely for that reason, they took on another dimension, at least in Maxi's mind. "Façade fantasies" always begin with a suspicion that treasures lie hidden, and the camouflage can be utterly banal. It was absurd to imagine literal treasures there, but in the depths of poverty, where money plays no role at all, other kinds of wealth emerge, for example the wealth of skills. This was intimated by the shantytown's wiring system. And there was no knowing what creative skills might have developed among people who had come from faraway places, and who, for the most part, had plenty of free time because they were unemployed.

There was another aspect of the layout that didn't conform to rational geometry, and that was the angle of the streets. If the overall shape of the shantytown was circular, then the streets should have run perpendicular to the edge, in a radial pattern, all converging at the center. But no: they ran off at an angle of forty-five degrees, all in the same direction (to the right, for someone facing inward). Which meant that none of them led to the center, or came out anywhere. Where did they end? Maxi never found out. His own incursions were limited to the outer rim; he went as far as the dwelling of the family he happened to be helping, but that was never more than a hundred yards in, always within sight of the perimeter. And since there were no cross streets, he had to go back out the same way. So the center, if indeed there was a center, remained a mystery to him. By the time he reached the shantytown it always seemed too late to ask about it, and he was too shy anyway. For some reason, the lighting, so lavish around the edge, diminished in intensity as one went further in, and toward the center the shantytown seemed to be quite dark. From this it might have been supposed that the middle was empty, but no: the density of settlement increased, the little streets became narrower and the shacks more tightly packed, although it was hard to see far. Even someone with good night vision would have found it difficult because the streets weren't exactly straight. As for Maxi, half asleep and practically blind (passing under the crown of light always left him dazzled), he would keep looking up and peering ahead as he hauled his load, and whether he was imagining things or misinterpreting what he saw, far off, on the way to the inaccessible center, he thought he could make out towers, domes, phantasmagoric castles, ramparts, pyramids, and groves.

Another thing that he had noticed was the abundance and variety of dogs: aloof, skinny, and mostly quite big. Luckily he wasn't one of those people who is afraid of dogs. Despite the late hour, they were out and about: rarely alone and sometimes in large packs, they came and went and slipped in everywhere, even running between his legs, or between the wheels of the cart. They were after food, presumably, and since it was so scarce, they had to keep searching night and day. No one paid them any attention or even noticed their existence. But they stayed near the edge, either outside the perimeter or in the first few yards of the little streets. Further in, they were rare, and Maxi never saw one heading for the inner depths or coming back.

III

IF MAXI HAD BEEN WORRIED (THOUGH HE NEVER WAS, not even for a moment) that someone he knew might see him with the collectors, he could have set his mind at rest. None of his friends or acquaintances ever saw him. This, perhaps, was partly due to chance, which sometimes chooses the path of abstention and follows it all the way through the intricate labyrinth of possibilities, and partly due to one of those blind spots that are so typical of big-city life. Not that he had gone completely unnoticed: someone had seen and recognized him. Only one person, who told no one else. And there was a reason why it should have been this person in particular: he was a policeman.

As I said before, Maxi lived on the corner of Bonorino and Bonifacio. Fifty yards away, on Calle Bonorino, was Police Station 38, and that's where Inspector Cabezas worked; he had been appointed to supervise the restructuring after the station had been taken over the previous year and all the senior officers dismissed (a judge had burst in one night, leading a special squad of judicial police, and discovered evidence that suspects were being tortured). Cabezas had completed that assignment a few months back but had continued to use the station, which was now functioning normally, as his personal headquarters. One night he saw Maxi hauling a collector's cart and recognized him. He'd often seen the kid coming out of the building on the corner and been struck his physique. But he would have recognized him anyway; his memory for faces was prodigious.

Once his curiosity was aroused, Cabezas began to keep an eye on Maxi. Since he didn't have to account for how he spent his time, he'd go out at night in his car, and was able to find Maxi without too much trouble. Cabezas would watch from a distance, sometimes parking for a while and sitting in the car, sometimes driving around the block, following the progress of the meathead and the scavengers. Before long he had more or less worked out Maxi's routine. At first he assumed that the kid was helping a particular family but he soon realized his mistake, and that intrigued him even more. On several occasions he followed Maxi into the depths of Lower Flores, to the end of his route, where he said goodbye to the collectors and set off home. A couple of times, late in the afternoon, he sat in his car, waiting for Maxi to step out into the street, then tailed him at a safe distance, keeping out of sight, all the way to the point at which he finally turned back, three or four hours later. The time this took was not an issue. Cabezas didn't do it every day; usually it was enough for him to catch a distant glimpse of Maxi, and see that he was still at it. Sometimes he let days and even whole weeks go by without checking, but then he returned to his observations.... And that was how he noticed Maxi getting closer to the shantytown. After the onset of winter, he would sometimes go to where Bonorino widened and wait for Maxi to stagger into view, at the end of his shift. One night he saw the boy actually go into the shantytown, which inflamed his curiosity and plunged him deep in thought.

Maxi and Inspector Cabezas were different in every way. In age, for a start. One was just beginning his adult life: he didn't know what he would do with it, and was always reacting on the basis of that uncertainty. The other had passed the age of fifty and begun his decline: he knew exactly what he'd done with his life, and took it for granted that the fabric of a man's destiny is woven by every one of his actions, no matter what his age. This was the source of a deep misunderstanding, which was to have serious consequences. The gulf between the two men was evident in the forms of their respective enterprises, which although superposed were incompatible. Maxi's was linear, an adventure open to improvisation, like a path disappearing into the distance. The inspector's enterprise, by contrast, resembled the deciphering of a structure. Policemen, whether or not they are influenced by detective fiction, tend to see things as aspects of a "case." As soon as Cabezas began to take an interest in Maxi's comings and goings, they constituted a case in his mind. Which meant that nothing could be left unexplained, and each explanation would have to be linked to others, to form a system, which in turn would have to be connected to other systems, until the whole of society was covered.

This was not a purely intellectual problem. In fact, Inspector Cabezas was not an intellectual at all. If an explanation was difficult to find, or he couldn't be bothered looking, he created one.

That's the way he was: a man of action, not a speculative thinker. And how do you "create" an explanation? By pressing on and improvising. In that respect his method did coincide with Maxi's, but at a different level and with different objectives. To him, "the case of the generous giant" was completely inexplicable, which gave him the widest possible scope for action. He had to create an explanation out of nothing, as it were.

The structure was based on real events: a rash of violence had broken out on the edge of that circular shantytown, known to the police as "the carousel." And the incidents had taken place precisely where Calle Bonorino widened out, which was also where the police station had once stood, long before. Providing, as ever, for fugitives and delinquents, the drug trade had intensified, raising the level of violence in the shantytowns, partly because of the serious money involved, but also because of the psychological disturbances produced by the drugs themselves. The situation in "the carousel" was particularly acute. And of course (this is where the inspector's procedure came in) it wasn't one case but a myriad, all of them interrelated. For instance, the violent trouble spot that was causing anxiety in the neighborhood didn't lie within the shantytown itself, where no one could be sure what was really going on, but outside, in its "vestibule."

That autumn, the newspaper *Clarín* had published a letter that read as follows: "Over recent years, the residents of 1800 Avenida Bonorino, in Lower Flores, have been subjected to an escalation of violence, instigated by a mafia whose headquarters are situated in the neighboring agglomeration of temporary dwellings. Firearms and drugs have become a daily presence in what was, until recently, a quiet working-class neighborhood, where children played in the streets. Now we live behind closed doors, day and night, held hostage in our own homes by rampant lawlessness. On the fifteenth of March, in an incident that is yet to be clarified, this deplorable situation lead to a fatality: a shot fired by an assault weapon ended the life of a fifteen-year-old girl. She was an outstanding student, her parents' pride and joy. She was my daughter. We are still waiting for an explanation; the culprits are still on the loose, terrorizing the local community; our family has been destroyed, and it is only a matter of time before this tragedy is repeated." Like all the readers' letters in the papers, it was signed, with an address (which was, predictably, 1800 Avenida Bonorino) and a National Identity Document number.

Inspector Cabezas had the cutting in his wallet, not because of its content—any number of such letters had been published—but because the signatory shared his surname: Cabezas. That, on its own, would not have been enough to make him cut the letter out and keep it, but the man's first name—Ignacio—was the same as well. This was a truly amazing coincidence because neither name was especially common. The inspector would have been very surprised just to learn that there was another Ignacio Cabezas, but the fact that his namesake also lived in Lower Flores, on his patch, and had made himself known to the public in that way, was something he could never have imagined, and it was enough to suggest the existence of a mechanism in which he had a part to play, though what that part might be he didn't know. He had been carrying the cutting around in his wallet for months, just in case, without showing it to anyone.

He had made no effort to meet the other Ignacio Cabezas, nor had he bothered to check the file on the killing because he knew what he would find. What interested him lay further afield, in the shantytown, which he had examined without, so far, discovering anything useful. Drugs were sold there in large quantities, everyone knew that, but no one knew how they came in and went out. It could have been done in a thousand ways. Long hours of surveillance, to which the inspector was accustomed, had revealed that buyers came at the oddest hours of the day or night, always in cars. They would pull up for a moment, ask something (what?), drive on again, and end up doing as many as ten full laps of the circular road that bounded the shantytown. It was extremely difficult to follow them without being noticed, especially at night, when there was no one else on the road, and it was brilliantly lit by the profusion of bulbs. The actual sales seemed to take place after dark; the daytime visits must have been exploratory. Cabezas was not the only one to have noticed; some of his colleagues had also been discreetly observing this activity, and they had come up with the apt and eloquent nickname, "the carousel."

The moment finally came to make use of that newspaper cutting. Cabezas knew that the meathead had a sister because he had seen the whole family coming out of the building on the corner, next to the police station. And he knew (police: what *don't* they know?) that the girl was mixed up with some bad sorts in the neighborhood. In fact, he had a more detailed picture of her than of her brother, who was a completely unknown quantity. So one day Cabezas followed her on foot, and waited until she was a fair way from home, in the middle of an empty block, before accosting her. He called out her name, and she turned around, alarmed. She was a pretty little blonde, with a sour look on her face. There was a chance that she'd recognize him; she might have seen him going into the station or coming out. But he decided to risk it because he knew how inattentive teenagers are, wrapped up in their own little worlds.

"I'm not trying to threaten you," he began. "I was going to talk with your parents, but then I thought we could come to an understanding, just the two of us. I don't want to upset them unnecessarily; I'm a father too, I know what it's like. They don't need to find out about anything, as long as you cooperate."

"Me? How? Who *are* you?"

The viper inside her reared up, but she couldn't hide the fact that she was nervous and afraid. "Gotcha, little whore," thought Cabezas.

"Do you have a minute?"

"No, I'm in a hurry."

"Here, read this," he said, giving her the cutting. This was such a strange and unexpected move that she found it paradoxically reassuring. The gesture itself was utterly familiar: the streets were full of jobless people handing out flyers. Except that it wasn't a flyer this time but a piece of newspaper. She looked at both sides and began to read. Although she maintained a neutral expression, Cabezas could tell, as he studied her face, that she knew what it was about and that her twisted little brain was getting to work. When he reckoned that she had reached the end, he pointed to the sender's name, and with his other hand held out his identity card, so she could see that the names were the same.

"That's right," he said, putting the cutting and the card back into his pocket, "I'm the father. For months now, I've been carrying out my own investigation; I wasn't going to hold my breath waiting for the police to do something. They're incompetent and corrupt," he added, to give his speech a touch of authenticity, sure to ring true for anyone who'd watched a bit of television. And to cover himself, in case she happened to see him entering or leaving the police station later on: "I go to Station 38 every day to see if there's any news, but they never do anything. I've found out all sorts of things, though, making my own inquiries." Here he paused and looked at her steadily. He could tell that she wanted to say, "And what's all this got to do with me?" but she couldn't because fear had paralyzed her lips.

"I know you used to see those layabouts from Commercial College Nine who went to the shantytown to buy proxidine. But don't worry, I'm not going to tell on you; like I said, I don't want to upset your parents unnecessarily. All I want is for you to help me find the bastards who killed my daughter. I quit my job so I could focus a hundred percent on finding them; it's all I think about ..."

"I never went to buy anything! I don't care who you tell!"

"I'm not going to tell anyone. I'm just asking you to have some compassion for a father in despair. Look, I know you didn't go to the shantytown to score. But you knew those kids; you used to hang out with them. People can do what they like, as far as I'm concerned. We're all free, and everyone wants drugs, that's obvious. What I said in the letter, it's not exactly true. I know my daughter was no saint, but that's no reason to kill her, is it?"

His question produced the desired effect. She nodded remorsefully.

"I want you to find out how the dealing is done in the shantytown. That's the only thing I haven't worked out, and until I do, I won't be able to unravel the mystery. I don't want you to tell me what you already know. You go ask your friends, as if you wanted to buy some yourself. I know where you live and where you go to school, and all the rest, so I'll be in touch. Remember this is a good deed you're doing. You help me, and I'll help you."

With that, he left her. He didn't think she'd be able to provide him with any useful information, though given the curious routes by which information circulates, who could tell? And anyhow, he was really after something else. He was happy with the way the conversation had gone. Next time, he'd be able to take it a bit further, and maybe he could even seduce her, while he was at it. Clearly, he was ignoring the old adage: "He who sleeps with children wakes up in a wet bed."

Vanessa was dazed and not exactly sure where she was, as if she'd been magically transported to a foreign city and didn't even know its name. Her little world was tottering. She started walking automatically, while her brain went into overdrive. But it was useless; she couldn't think about anything. Or rather, there was just one thing she could think about; and she thought about it so intensely that it left no room for anything else: she had to find help. She was the kind of person who needs help all the time, for everything. And now more than ever before. Except that now her need, it seemed, had exceeded the bounds of the possible: she needed more help than heaven and earth could provide. And yet—so strange are the workings of the mind—the ideal person occurred to her immediately, someone who, five minutes earlier, could not have been further from her thoughts.

This providential person was a maid who worked in the building directly opposite her apartment. Although they had never spoken, Vanessa knew that the girl lived in the shantytown and walked up from there every morning. She'd also seen her with one of those dangerous Bolivian drug dealers. The maid looked Bolivian too, and Vanessa might have been getting her mixed up because to her all Bolivians looked the same. Only someone in a state of high agitation would have resorted to such an unlikely source of help, but the girl was there, just across the street, and that was enough for Vanessa. She turned around and went straight back home; it was the ideal time to make contact. She'd be alone, and from the front window she'd be able to see if the maid was cleaning as usual. Maybe she'd be alone too, and they would be able to talk.

Vanessa went upstairs and rushed to the window. Across the street, the doors that opened onto the balconies were closed, but the curtains were open; she could see into the bedrooms: no one there. She went to the telephone and only then did she realize that she didn't know the number. That didn't matter. There was a way she could find out: her best friend lived in the same building. She called the friend, who wasn't home, but her mother answered and gave Vanessa the surname of the people who owned the third-floor apartment. She searched frenetically in the phone book. Among all the entries for that name, there was one with the address 200 Bonorino. She called the number. A woman's voice answered.

"I want to speak with the maid who's working there," she said.

"Who's speaking?"

The accent was funny. It must have been her.

"It's you, isn't it?"

"Ma'am, yes."

Vanessa heaved a sigh of relief, as if all her problems were over.

"Listen, I'm the girl who lives in the apartment on the third floor of the building opposite, I always see you in the window. You must have seen me."

A silence.

"Hello!"

"Ma'am, yes. Who?"

"Opposite, directly opposite! I'm at the window now. Can you use the phone in one of the bedrooms. It's very important. If you go to one of the bedrooms you'll see me. I can see into the bedrooms from here."

"Ma'am, yes."

Another silence.

"Hello!"

Nothing. Had she understood? Vanessa fixed her gaze on the balconies. After an eternity, she saw the girl appear, as black as a cockroach, as small as a ten-year old, and pick up the phone from a bedside table.

"Ma'am, yes."

"Hello! Here I am. Look straight ahead." She opened the window with one hand and waved her arm desperately. "Can you see me? No, look this way! Outside!"

Vanessa saw her turn slowly, like a sleepwalker (or was it an effect of the distance?) and look all around.

"Can you see me? I live here, right opposite. Hello! Hello!" These *hellos* were accompanied by extravagant arm gestures.

"Ma'am, yes."

"Don't call me Ma'am, you're not talking to my mom, it's me. Can you see me now? Do you see where I am?"

"Ma'am ... yes."

"Listen, what's your name?"

"Ma'am, Adela."

"Adela, my name's Vanessa. I've been seeing you around for a while, and I know you live down near 1800 Bonorino." She thought it would be tactless to say "in the shantytown." "One time I saw you coming up from there with the fat man who used to hang out with the kids from Commercial College Nine."

"Who? What man?"

"A short, fat guy. A man, or a boy, I don't know." As well as being unable to tell those people apart, she couldn't tell what age they were. "He had a bright red jacket. Anyway, it doesn't matter. That's not what I wanted to tell you. I'm desperate. This guy just stopped me in the street: the father of the girl that got shot at 1800 Bonorino. He's crazy! He wants to kill them all! I don't know what to do. He's after me, he knows where I live, he's harassing me. If my parents find out, they'll kill me ..."

She was out of control, sobbing and talking so quickly it was incomprehensible. Adelita seemed to be puzzled, with good reason.

"But what do you want?"

"For you to fucking sort it out! I'm being harassed by a madman ... and I've got nothing to do with it! I've never even been there. I saw that fat guy once in my whole life. I don't know who he is. You must know, that's why I called you."

"Ma'am, I don't know …"

"I want this to finish now! Now! I don't want anything more to do with it." She was losing control again, crying so much she couldn't even speak. In the end they hung up.

Adelita stood there pensively. The lady of the house came into the bedroom.

"Who called you?"

"Ma'am, the girl who lives across the street: she's crazy! She was staring at me through the window as she talked! There she is, can you see?" The lady turned and saw the girl, standing by the phone in the apartment opposite, weeping convulsively. Luckily, Vanessa didn't look up and see how her secret had begun to spread as soon as it had left her mouth.

"But what's wrong?" asked the lady. "Why did she call you?"

"Ma'am, she says that she's being harassed by the father of that girl who was killed in my neighborhood."

The lady looked horrified.

"When is this nightmare going to end? And does she know …"

"Ma'am, no," said Adelita, making an effort to compose her features because now she was beginning to feel upset. "She thinks I know the people who sell drugs. She said she saw me coming up the street with …"

"With who?"

"I think she meant the Pastor. She mentioned that shiny red jacket he has."

"Mmm … and when did you come up with the Pastor?"

"One day, it only happened once; I ran into him on the way up. He was going to the police station, Ma'am; it's the only time I've ever talked with him. He asked me if I lived in the neighborhood, if I believed in Jesus, and then he went on and on."

"Typical," remarked the lady, disdainfully. "It's a wonder he didn't ask where you work, and whether your employers believe in Jesus Christ, and what kind of car they have ..."

Adelita couldn't stop herself smiling:

"Ma'am, I think he did."

"I hope you didn't tell him!" said the lady, laughing. "What a nosy little shit!" She stopped to think for a moment. "Life is so strange. You talk with a guy in the street just once; somebody sees you and assumes that you're friends."

"What a coincidence, Ma'am Élida ..."

It really was surprising. Not so much the business with the Pastor, a self-styled evangelical minister, who preached in the shanty-town and extracted money from the gullible, but only as a cover for his real, paid job, as a police informant. The "coincidence" to which Adelita had referred, picking up on the word "nightmare," used earlier by her employer, was that her boyfriend had been implicated in the death of that poor girl, and the following day, the sixteenth of March, he had disappeared. Nobody had seen him since. It wasn't clear what had happened, what kind of accident had led to the firing of the fatal shot. Adelita was sure that her boyfriend was innocent, maybe just a witness, or not even that. But the fact was that he had vanished, without telling anyone where he was going: not his friends, not his parents (with whom he lived), not even her. He was a timid, gentle boy, incapable of hurting a fly, almost excessively childlike and shy. He'd probably been so disturbed by the death that he'd run away in a blind panic, with no idea where he was going. No shock should have lasted that long, but with him it was hard to tell; perhaps he was more fragile than Adelita had thought. She had cried and cried, and looked in all the places where she imagined he might be hiding; she kept visiting his parents at regular intervals to see if they had any news. But there was no sign of him. People from his village in Peru had told her that he hadn't gone back there. The world was so big. . . .

They had been good together: they were outwardly similar, "made for each other," but she had the energy and strength of character that he lacked. She was just what a boy like him would need, when he became a man: someone who'd always be there for him, supportive but inconspicuous. Over the weeks and months that followed his disappearance, Adelita had resigned herself to never seeing him again. She'd even found a new boyfriend and they'd gone dancing a couple of times before she decided that she didn't really like him. Naturally she had told her employers everything. Mornings she looked after Madame Élida's apartment, and afternoons she worked for one of Élida's sisters-in-law, cleaning her home and business. Both women had offered support and advice, especially Élida, who was like a mother to her. Emerging now from a private daydream and returning to the topic of Vanessa, Élida said:

"I know her mother. We sometimes chat in the street and she's told me about the trouble they've been having with that little brat. Next time I see her, I'll tell her about the phone call, just so she knows."

"Ma'am ..." said Adelita in a murmur and went back to her work, but now she was weeping silently. An old wound had re-opened. It was possible, even probable, that her boyfriend, Alfredo, had used the opportunity provided by the crime and his vague association with it to get away from her. He wouldn't have had the courage to take that step under normal circumstances, but fate had provided him with an easy way out. He really was shy and awkward; he didn't know how to talk to girls. Somehow he'd plucked up the courage to start a conversation with her, but maybe that was just because she was ugly and insignificant. ...
He was good looking, though, and in the end he must have realized that he could do better; but because of his shyness and inexperience, he couldn't find a way to break it off. Maybe that was what had happened. Deep down Adelita suspected as much, and it hurt.

That's how she was: unassuming, serious, responsible, conscientious. She kept no secrets from anyone, and yet her life was surrounded by mystery. Nobody can tell what lives in the heart of a girl like her. Poor and small as she was, she had her own personal genie, not the standard guardian angel that other people believe in, but a supernatural masculine being of extraordinary proportions, who accompanied her everywhere, protecting her twenty-four hours a day, always wide awake even when she was sleeping. Nothing like those effeminate angels: a giant at least twenty yards tall, with a powerful chest ten yards wide. When he stretched out his arms he was the size of an enormous tree. How could any man approach her, once he had noticed that presence? Which showed how blind that ridiculous "Pastor" was. A wonder the giant hadn't smacked him dead on the spot. Not that men were forbidden, as long as they didn't have ulterior motives. She wasn't planning to be left on the shelf. On the contrary. The plan was to find love.

While all this was happening on the third floor, up on the fifth, a girl called Jessica came home, and was told by her mother that Vanessa, her friend from across the street, had called to find out the surname of the people who lived downstairs. This plunged Jessica into a turmoil of speculation. She knew what a scheming piece of work Vanessa was (they'd fallen out, and it was extremely surprising that she'd called). Something fishy was going on, and Jessica resolved to find out what.

Cabezas would have been surprised to learn that the effects of his Machiavellian initiative were spreading like the proverbial wildfire. He was blinkered: he couldn't see beyond the structure and its realization. This limitation had worked for him so far, and he had come to believe that it always would. His mistake was thinking that a battle is fought at a single point in space. That is not the case. A battle always covers a large area, and none of the participants can take it in at a glance, not even retrospectively. Nobody can grasp the whole, mainly because in reality there is no whole to be grasped.

Something similar applies to time. The inspector's error in that regard was a little more justifiable, since, as a policeman, he was supposed to be "an agent of justice" and in that capacity he had to believe that his work was underpinned by a transcendent rationale.

How mistaken he was! If God intervened in earthly justice, crimes would be punished straight away. And that could only happen if it had been happening all along, in which case human beings would have adjusted their behavior accordingly. People would refrain from robbing and killing just as they get out of the way of a speeding bus: they would do it automatically because the species would have incorporated the knowledge that the consequences were automatic and fatal. In other words, it wouldn't be strictly speaking a matter of deliberation and choice. But in the world as we know it, God waits. When moral rather than physical laws are operating, time has to pass between the act and its consequences. And in that lapse of time other things happen.

In the case at hand, someone was presumably responsible for the death of the young woman, and time had passed without the culprit receiving any punishment. That lapse of time was not empty: time never is, nor can it be. And the strangest thing is that what happens in the meantime is odd and unexpected too—that is, the intervening events occur in a fortuitous order; sometimes the effects even come before the causes.... But since time is defined by an orderly causal chain of events, if cause and effect change places, it's as if time were abolished. (Here it should be mentioned that the "Pastor," whom Maxi's sister had mistaken for a drug boss, had chosen the imminent End of the World as the theme for his preaching that year.)

IV

FROM THE FIFTH FLOOR, JESSICA HAD SEEN VANESSA crying by the phone and this made her so curious that she went back to the kitchen to question her mother. What had Vanessa said when she called? Why did she want the name of the people on the third floor?

"How should I know?" said her mother, who was making stuffed zucchinis. "I already told you I didn't ask. I gave her the name and she hung up."

"And how do you know their name?"

Just the sort of question a teenager would ask: she was so absorbed in her own little world she couldn't imagine how anyone would know the neighbors' names.

"But darling, why *wouldn't* I? We've been here fifteen years. I always have a chat with the lady when I see her downstairs or in the elevator …"

"And you asked her name?"

"Of course not, but it's on the list of co-proprietors, the bills, her mail, lots of places. You just end up knowing these things in a condo; it's not like you have to investigate."

"Which one is she?"

"Huh?"

"That lady, the one from the third floor."

"You must have seen her thousands of times; she's the one with wavy, dyed-red hair, who walks slowly and always wears really high heels." Jessica tried to place her, but couldn't. Her mother sighed: it was hopeless. "She's called Élida, her husband's a fat, pasty-faced guy with glasses. They have a white Duna, and their carport is right next to ours."

"Cars are all the same to me."

"You should pay more attention."

"And why did Vanessa want their name?"

"Where's your head?! How many times do I have to tell you I don't know!" Jessica's mother regretted this outburst immediately. But the girl was trying her patience with those childlike questions. "Call her and ask."

"But we're not talking."

"Well, she called you."

"No. She called *you*."

"No. She called you. She said: Is Jessica in? I said: No, she's gone out. She'll be back in a minute. Ah, she said, Can you do me a favor then? The people who live on the third floor in your building, what's their name? Gandulla, I said. And then she hung up straight away. I've got no idea why she wanted to know!"

"Maybe to look up the name in the directory and call them."

"What directory? The telephone directory? Yes, maybe. But no. Because I didn't give her the first name, just the surname, and there must be lots of Gandullas in the directory."

They thought about this for a while. Jessica shook her head

despondently, but then a possibility occurred to her mother:

"She could have used the address."

"How do you mean used the address?" asked Jessica. "Are there addresses in the directory?"

"Yes. Haven't you ever noticed? You're so vague, it's incredible."

"But if she was using the address to find the number, why did she need the name?"

Her mother took a deep mental breath and explained:

"In the directory the names are arranged in alphabetical order. She found the name Gandulla, then she looked for the Gandulla who lives at this address. Do you get it now?"

"Yes."

"Anyway, you're just guessing that she looked in the directory. Maybe she wasn't trying to call them; maybe she needed the name for some other reason."

"No! She must have called them! I saw her crying like anything right next to the phone."

Jessica's mother turned to look at her, intrigued.

"Seriously?"

"Yes! She was crying with her face in her hands, like this."

"How do you know she was crying? You saw her from across the street, through the windows, with all the reflections. How can you be so sure? Maybe she was laughing."

"No, I know her." Her tone of voice had changed, as if a thought had occurred to her. Jessica's mother noticed this; she knew her daughter well. She also knew that there was no point trying to make her say what it was. Meanwhile, she'd had a thought of her own. To get the lay of the land, she said:

"Maybe she wanted to tell them that something had fallen onto their balcony or that something was hanging out a window, or whatever. Something she'd noticed. I mean she does live directly opposite, on the same floor ..."

Jessica was lost in her own thoughts and it took her a while to process this conjecture. But her reaction, when it came, was impatient:

"No. What would she care? Why would that make her cry?"

"Maybe they were rude to her on the phone. It's awful when you're just trying to help and someone tells you to mind your own business."

"Come on, Mom, that makes *no* sense!"

Jessica's mother concentrated on her zucchini for a moment. The sky had clouded over, and the light coming into the kitchen was gentler. The cream-colored tiles went right up to the ceiling and everything was tidy and spotlessly clean. Eventually she decided to say what she was thinking:

"Listen, Jessica, I don't know what's going on—you know I've never liked Vanessa—but I suspect she's up to something."

"Why?" said her daughter defensively, almost too defensively.

"You must have heard us, your father and me, talking about Mr. Gandulla (though you were probably daydreaming); anyway, this Gandulla, Élida's husband, has a series of big properties scattered around Buenos Aires, and some evangelical church uses them for worship. One day your father tried to pump him, and he said he just rented the buildings to the ministers and had nothing to do with the church himself. But then he said that he was buying properties in strategic locations, and fitting them out, and that he also had a fleet of buses to transport the congregations, and houses and sports fields for church activities. So he's involved; he's not just renting a few properties. Did you know that?"

"No, I had no idea."

"What about Vanessa?"

"No, no way."

"But she might have found out and maybe that's why she wanted to talk with the Gandullas."

Jessica could not have been more completely or sincerely surprised. The mere idea that Vanessa might be taking an interest in religion left her speechless. But her mother still had an ace up her sleeve:

"What I'm thinking is, one of the church's projects is a rehabilitation program for young addicts. They have at least two rehab farms on the outskirts of Buenos Aires. It's supposed to be a charity, but who knows what kind of operation they're really running out there. Mirta from the second floor is good friends with Élida, and she's told me all sorts of things. For example: Gandulla is buddies with the superintendent at the police station across the street, so whenever they pick up kids on drugs they send them straight to one of those farms."

"And what's this got to do with Vanessa?"

"That's what I'm wondering, darling. The state she was in when you saw her crying, it must be something serious. You don't have any idea?"

"What? How would I know? You're crazy! You never give up, do you?"

"I'm going to have a word with Vanessa's mother and warn her. Next time I see her I'll say something.... After all, I don't know why you two aren't talking anymore."

Jessica got up and stormed out, yelling:

"I've had it up to here with you! Always sticking your nose in...!"

She went to her bedroom, slammed the door behind her, rushed to the sliding glass doors that opened onto the balcony and looked out. The windows of Vanessa's apartment were dark and empty. Since she was looking down from above, all she could see was a strip of floor. When their friendship had been running smoothly, Vanessa used to come to the window, and they would talk on the phone, looking at each other. The circumstances that had led to Jessica's decision to go out shopping and therefore caused her to miss the call filled her now with an irrational hatred. She felt powerless in the face of time, paralyzed, yet deeply unsettled. It was almost as if her whole life had been one big mistake, and there was nothing she could do to correct it. Her mother's suppositions weren't even worth considering; they were too ridiculous, too fictional. She could make a better job of it and come up with something far more realistic: all she had to do was to think and react in her usual way, in other words, be herself. Because deep down she and Vanessa were the same: each was capable of anything the other one might do. And yet, strangely, when she set about testing this method of "being herself," she didn't feel herself at all.

Vanessa, she thought, had obviously wanted to talk to her. She'd been impelled by some mysterious but irresistible desire. Not because she wanted to make peace, or negotiate, or continue the quarrel with fresh accusations, but for some other reason unknown to Jessica (neither of them knew, nor could have known, what it was). When she hadn't been able to get through, she'd made up any old excuse to justify the call, the first thing that came into her head: asking for the name of the neighbors on the third floor, whose apartment was right in front of her. And when she'd hung up and realized that the call had been a fiasco, she'd broken down crying. Jessica could understand that too, especially since she felt that she was about to burst into tears herself. None of it made any sense, even if she could make sense of it.

She was standing there looking at the façade of the building opposite. The two buildings were mirror images of each other. They had been built by the same construction company and were identical down to the last detail, not just on the outside, but in the internal layout of the apartments too. The balconies were full of plants, with big festoons of foliage spilling down to the balconies below. The windows reflected the building across the street: Vanessa's building reflected Jessica's, and vice versa. And an attentive observer with a sharp eye would no doubt have been able to see a reflection within the reflection, and so on ad infinitum, as with mirrors set up face to face.

To think that when Vanessa called, she was coming up in the elevator! It was such a close thing, a matter of seconds! And the way Vanessa had burst into tears, she knew the feeling exactly: an overwhelming surge made up of all the situation's little details. That's what life was always like: miniscule, intangible accidents combining to form an immense emotion bigger than life itself. And that was the transcendental justification for the girls' notorious frivolity; if her mother had been able to understand this, she wouldn't have had to come up with such far-fetched explanations.

Suddenly, Jessica's heart stopped. Her breathing too, and her thinking. She froze like a movie still, pressed against the glass, all eyes. Across the street, on the third floor, Vanessa had appeared. When someone you've been thinking about intensely appears and is there in front of you, it seems incredible, at least for the first moment, before you begin to communicate, and the mind is otherwise occupied. On this occasion, however, there was no communication because Vanessa didn't look at Jessica but left her in a state of pure contemplation, trapped, that is, in the initial moment, confined within herself. Nobody likes being left out. An involuntary expression of horror came over Jessica's face.

Vanessa didn't look up once. She was staring straight ahead. It was Vanessa all right, but somehow—and this was the scariest thing—it wasn't. She was very pale, "white as a sheet," except her nose and around her eyes, where the skin was a bright carmine color. She looked like a clown with her face painted white and red. And the face, although still hers, was not a face: it had no outer surface, it was hollowed or sharpened, almost concave. The eyes were independent of it, staring straight ahead, like those of a robot. Her body seemed to be hanging from her gaze, and its stiffness suggested a superhuman determination, as if thought could no longer act upon it, only gravity. For a moment, Jessica had the horrific impression that she was about to jump. "She's going to jump!" And there was nothing she could do! That tiny shift in time was going to be what killed her. Jessica looked away in anguish, not to find help but because her eyes were the only part of her body that she could move. And she saw a little black figure in the glass door that opened onto the balcony of the apartment just above Vanessa's. The size of this figure intrigued her: it was too small. A little human figure making gratuitous circular movements, as if performing a strange dance without music, in a space where it didn't belong, midway between floor and ceiling. It took Jessica a while to realize that what she was seeing was a reflection of someone in her own building.

She half-closed her eyes, keeping them fixed on the unidentified figure, who must have been below her, on the third floor, and was, she now realized, the object of Vanessa's spellbound stare. What her mother had said about that mysterious third floor came back to her like a tidal wave and swept all her earlier thoughts away. But what was she doing, that woman in black, moving back and forth within a tiny space, as if she were inside a bubble? Was it Élida, the lady her mother chatted with? No, it was a girl . . . and those little steps backward and forward, opening and closing her arms. She looked like a doll in a music box. Finally Jessica worked it out: they were the movements of someone who is cleaning a room: making the bed, tidying up, vacuuming. The room must have been full of light, and she was wearing black; that's why only her figure was visible. And that explained who she was: the maid. And perhaps it also explained why Vanessa was watching her with such interest. But why would Vanessa care about how that room was being cleaned? What did that have to do with religion? Maybe it was true that she had tried to call that apartment. For some deeply mysterious reason involving religion and housekeeping. And then the crying, the captivated stupor . . .

Jessica looked at her friend again. Vanessa was still there, frozen. She lifted her gaze to the reflected figure, then let it drop back to Vanessa. She was beginning to breathe again. The horror was gradually receding, but deepening as well and expanding enormously. Up until now she had been assuming that *she* was Vanessa's secret. Her interpretation of this strange scene had been entirely based on that assumption. But nobody owned the secret: it could detach itself from individuals and take over the world, and then there'd be no hope of understanding anything.

She couldn't make out the face of the girl in the reflection, but she didn't need to. Her silhouette, her movements and her general aura were as unique as the features of a face. And they reminded Jessica of someone, irresistibly. She knew who it was: Cynthia, the girl who got killed, Cynthia Cabezas. Poor Vanessa! She'd seen Cynthia from her apartment and panicked. But how could a dead girl be there, on the third floor, making the beds? And not just that: the really unbelievable thing was that Cynthia, a student at Misericordia, like them, was working as a maid, even if she *was* dead. But if the owners of that apartment belonged to an esoteric cult, maybe they were using dead people as slaves.... Vanessa had discovered their secret, and now she didn't know what to do. Jessica resolved to intervene, though she wasn't sure how. It had to be something properly planned, she couldn't simply improvise. In spite of everything, she almost smiled to see how fragile reason was: Vanessa's had crumbled at the first blow, all she'd been able to do was reach for the phone, like a castaway grasping at a plank.

V

RAPT, IN THE PINK WINTER DUSK, MAXI WAS CONTEM-
plating something ... something without a name. Action. Or
silence. But no, it really didn't have a name. And then, in the
depths of the inexpressible, the work that he had invented began
like a melody. Was it work? A service? A way to give meaning to
his strength and free time? Or was it nothing at all? It was like
someone making a job out of giving up his seat on the bus. Doing
a favor for a stranger in the street is, essentially, a spontaneous,
unpremeditated act, almost an improvisation; in any case, not
planned ahead, and impossible to integrate into a program. And
yet that was what Maxi seemed to have done. But not exactly or
entirely. His action hovered in a kind of ambiguity. For a start, it
didn't have a clear purpose. And any purpose it might have had
was determined not by him but by the nature of the scavengers'
work. The scavengers themselves were not an eternal given; their
very existence was contingent and depended on historical circumstances. Rummaging through garbage is not something that
people do out of a sense of vocation: a little socioeconomic shift
would have been enough to provide them all with alternative oc-
cupations. But there they were: rummaging through garbage! It

was as if they had adapted instantaneously, from one day to the next. Perhaps sudden adaptations like that were more frequent than they seemed; perhaps they were the norm. And they must have been occurring at many levels, on one of which a niche had opened up for Maxi, who, in his way, had also effected an adaptation, or something similar: he had transfigured an impulsive, spontaneous gesture into a way of occupying time.

For someone as sensitive as he was to the passing hours of the day, the winter dusk was bound to have a meaning. But what was it? The meaning without a name, in other words: nothing. The meanings all fell away, or revealed how empty they had been from the start. Hardly anything happens, after all, in an individual life: most of the time is spent working to survive and then recovering from work. If someone added up all the time that individuals have spent achieving nothing, just to keep time ticking over, the sum total of centuries and millennia would be overwhelming. By comparison, history is a miniature. But history is a condensation of facts, an intellectual contrivance that artificially gathers together the little that happened in the vast, half-empty expanses of real time.

The time of day was merely a signal for what was about to begin: the reverse of Maxi's life, the night. His body eclipsed his consciousness, and from that point on he knew nothing. He didn't know what happened at night. Against the background of that old ignorance, a newer one emerged: how did the inhabitants of the shantytown manage to survive? He understood the collectors' system more or less, or could have (if he'd made a more concerted effort), but there weren't many of them—a dozen, or two dozen, three at the most—and there were tens of thousands of families living in the shantytown. What did they live on? Air? He couldn't rule it out. Maybe you didn't need so much to live. Extending the earlier reasoning, it might be supposed that the moments at which you actually need something from outside to maintain your place in society or humanity are sparsely scattered over large empty stretches of time in which it is possible to manage with nothing. Added together, those moments of need would come to two or three minutes per year, and there's always a way to get through such a short span of time.

Anyway, what poor people? The few he saw (by the time he entered the shantytown, the doors were closing) looked and behaved like any other Argentines. The only thing that identified them as poor was living in those makeshift dwellings. It's true that no one chooses to live in a shantytown, but had he chosen to live where he did? And was it really so obvious that no one would prefer that kind of poverty? Perhaps not when faced with an actual choice, but some might find it desirable in a speculative way. Those dollhouse-like constructions had their charm, precisely because of their fragility and their thrown-together look. To appreciate that charm one only had to be sufficiently frivolous. Maxi wasn't, but for him, the houses had another advantage: they simplified things enormously. For someone wearied or overwhelmed by the complexities of middle-class life, they could seem to offer a solution. Since their owners had made them, they could just as easily tear them down or leave them behind. After a day, a week, or a year, when the house had served its purpose, the owners could continue on their way. Or rather, make their way.... Of course, for this system to work you had to know how to make a house, of a rudimentary kind, at least. And who knows that? Poor people, that's who. It sets them apart, and maybe it's what makes them poor.

There was a moment each night when Maxi found himself alone in the shantytown. He would relinquish the handles and let the cart's owners take over; they would head off between walls of tin, vanishing after the briefest goodbye, or before. They never invited him into their homes, understandably. He felt as if he were waking up, as if something were about to start. But it was time to finish, to go home, have dinner and sleep. He could barely keep his eyes open or walk straight; his perception was closing down like a clam. Otherwise, it would have been a perfect opportunity to explore. When he went down one of those diagonal streets, he always stayed fairly close to the edge of the shantytown, in the part that was brightly lit. Above his head were strings of light bulbs forming circles, squares, triangles, rows: a different pattern in every street. He kept looking back over his shoulder. Behind him, he could see the white light of Avenida Bonorino; ahead, darkness. The inner depths of the shantytown disappeared into the shadows, and that, along with his sleepiness, discouraged him from venturing further. And then there was the fact that the streets didn't lead to the center. Because of the angle at which they ran, they would miss it, however far they went. In fact, they led *away* from the center, not just certain streets but all of them. In the end, he would turn around and head for home.

The shantytown wasn't deserted. There were people about, of course: he was surrounded on all sides by a veritable ocean of

humanity. And the people weren't invisible. They did tend to go
inside at that time of night, mainly because of the cold, and close
their doors, or the sheets of tin or cardboard that they used as
doors, but there were still some people walking around, or looking out, or hurrying home, or setting off for somewhere. No one
paid him any attention; they didn't even seem to see him. He
didn't look at them much either; he didn't want to come across as
a sightseer, or a busybody; anyway, he was shy, and by that time
of night he wasn't up to noticing anything much.

Nevertheless, one night, at that moment of hesitation when
he was left alone and turned his gaze, as usual, toward the inte-
rior of the shantytown, he noticed a barely visible figure further
down the little street and stayed to watch as it emerged from the
darkness, becoming clearer with every step. There was nothing
special about that figure, no reason for it to intrigue him, and yet
he stood there rooted to the spot, staring. Had he sensed that his
gaze was being returned by someone who knew him, and was
coming to say hello? Sometimes you can know that much before
you know anything else. If so, he should, in turn, have recognized
the figure, and he did have a hunch of a sort, growing stronger
by the moment. The identification of a tiny moving silhouette,
barely distinct from the shadows, seemed an impossible task.
But subliminal recognition at a distance is not so unusual either.
Because of his poor night vision, Maxi was accustomed to the
tricks of perception but also to its exploits. There was an asym-
metry because he was right underneath a crown of bulbs, bathed
in light, and the unknown figure was still coming out of the darkness, as if dragging it along behind. Was it a man or a woman?

Actually, it looked like a child. Or rather it seemed too small to be real, even taking the distance into account.

A feeling of exaltation suddenly took hold of Maxi. Suddenly it seemed to him that the depths of the shantytown were about to reveal a small part of their great mystery. Why he felt this, he didn't know. Perhaps just because the figure was coming from that direction and must have known what was there and was coming to tell him. This last supposition was unfounded. But it was possible and that was enough. And it wasn't the only possibility in play. Wouldn't it be wonderful if it was someone he knew, so they could say hello, and chat as they left the shantytown together! Even if it was somebody he barely knew at all, practically a stranger, it wouldn't matter. Although it was true that something like that would have to be a miracle.

Anyone with normal eyesight would already have been able to see the person's face. Maxi had to wait until the figure came within ten yards to realize that it was a girl: a very thin, short girl, with practically no breasts or hips, completely dressed in black, wearing tight pants, with her hair tied back. There was a big, flat patch of red swinging beside her. It was a garment, a coat or a raincoat, in a transparent plastic bag, the way they wrap them at the dry-cleaner's. When he looked up again, he could see her face. She was a girl with Indian features, a boyish look and a deeply serious expression that seemed to be permanent. And yet, when she came up to him, she smiled, and although the smile was very brief, it was very encouraging, mostly because it came as a surprise. Maxi plucked up the courage to greet her with a "Hi," which she did not return. He didn't know how to talk to girls, he could never come up with anything to say. But she did reply in the end, and he fell into step beside her. After all, they were going in the same direction.

"Sir, are you going home?"

"Yes, it's late already."

"Sir, it's not so late."

"For me it is. Very late!"

Then there was a silence, and fearing that it would go on forever, Maxi said the first thing that came into his head, in a brusque tone that he began to regret even as the words came out of his mouth:

"What are you up to at this time of night?"

"Sir, I'm going to buy food for dinner."

"Now? Why don't you go to the supermarket and shop for the whole week? It works out cheaper."

He'd put his foot in his mouth again! Poor people live day by day, obviously; they don't stock up for a week or a month, and anyway there are no supermarkets in shantytowns. But she didn't take offence, and said exactly what Maxi's mother would have said:

"Sir, there's always something you need at the last minute."

"You're not afraid to be out alone at night?"

"Sir, I'm with you now."

"Yes, because you ran into me by chance. You could get mugged for a peso round here." He realized that it was rude to talk like that about the people who lived in the shantytown, but it was better than letting her think that he had been imagining the possibility of rape. Attempting to cancel the bad impression, he made a more general comment: "It's shameful that people who have almost nothing will rob each other of the little they have."

"Sir, I don't think it's so bad."

"What!? So you justify theft? You'd steal too, would you?"

"Sir, can you see me trying to mug someone? They'd laugh in my face." And it was true: she was scrawny. "What I mean is, if someone can steal, let him steal. If that's what he's made for, what else is he supposed to do? Especially if an opportunity arises."

"That's the law of the jungle," said Maxi, shaking his head despondently.

"Sir, all I know is that everyone looks out for their own interests, and they can only do it properly if they exploit all their relative advantages, legal or not, otherwise they'll lose out."

"But someone else will win!"

"Sir, that's right, but the thing is, for the overall balance to be maintained, everyone has to exploit their possibilities to the maximum! Otherwise there'd be gaps. If I don't do something that I could do, because of a scruple, I'm relying on other people acting in the same way, and how can I know that they will? How can I oblige them to have the same kind of scruples as me? This is the source of much bitterness."

She spoke with quite a strong accent, which Maxi couldn't identify, but it had the merit of making her words, and even the situation, plausible. He bent down toward her and said:

"That's what I mean by 'the law of the jungle': everything for me, nothing for the others."

"Sir, if everyone says the same thing, then everyone will have everything. We are all 'me.'"

"You don't really think that," he said, in a brusque tone again, as if he were impatient or cross, although he wasn't: it was just a way of talking, quite common among the shy. And as before, he broke the ensuing silence with a generalization: "There shouldn't be any poor people."

She shrugged her shoulders imperceptibly:

"What poor people? Sir, that's an old-fashioned word. In the old days, there were poor people and rich people because there was a world made up of the poor and the rich. Now that world has disappeared, and the poor have been left without a world. That's why the ladies I work for say: 'There are no poor people anymore.'"

"But there are."

"Sir, yes. You only have to look around."

"And they must suffer as a result," Maxi hazarded.

"Sir, I'm not sure. The old world of rewards and punishments is finished. Now it's just a question of living. It doesn't matter how."

"I just thought of something—maybe you'll think it's crazy. Imagine that a poor man comes across a rich man; he pulls out a knife and steals all the cash the rich man is carrying, and his watch while he's at it. OK. Then they go their separate ways. And what happens? What happens is the rich man goes on being rich, and the poor man goes on being poor. So what use was the robbery? None at all. It's like it never happened. You probably think that's stupid."

"Sir, it's a thought that must have occurred to many other people because there's a story I've often heard, sir, which starts in the same way: a poor man comes across a rich man, and attacks him

... and from that moment on, the poor man is rich, and the rich man poor, forever."

"I've never heard that."

It struck him as a typical "poor person's story." Or a typical "rich person's story." Once a story gets to be typical, the differences dissolve. Since he belonged to neither group, it wasn't surprising he'd never heard it.

At this point in the conversation, he became uncomfortably aware of an uncertainty that often bothers people with a poor memory for faces: did he know his interlocutor? They must have known each other from somewhere, otherwise she wouldn't have engaged him so naturally in conversation. There was an additional difficulty because in this case he couldn't really blame his poor memory for faces: with a girl like her, the face was neither here nor there. His memory would have treated her as a social and human whole. He didn't have the energy to run through all the possibilities, so he gave up trying to place her. If he didn't want to make a fool of himself, or worse, hurt the feelings of this innocent girl, he had to maintain the ambiguity, which limited what they could talk about. Maybe the limits had been in place from the start, and that was how they'd got onto poverty.

As if she had guessed what he was thinking, she said:

"Here in Flores, we all know each other, even if it's only by sight."

"Really? You know everyone?"

"Sir, if I tried to keep something hidden, people would find out. There's always someone watching, no matter where you go. And you can't go very far, of course, unless you take a bus."

"...?"

"I was thinking of what you said before, about getting mugged."

"Oh, that."

"Sir, someone would see the thieves and go tell the police."

"As if they'd care!"

"Sir, you never know what they'll care about."

They had reached the road and come to a halt. Maxi looked at the large red garment suspended from the girl's hand. Then he looked back down the little street. Lights arranged in the shape of a star were shining above it. He thought: "This is her street. I must remember the star."

"I don't think anyone pays much attention to me," he said.

"Sir, but people do! You don't realize.... That's what I wanted to tell you. Someone saw you come here and went to threaten your sister."

"My sister? Why?"

"Because he thinks that her friends come here to buy drugs."

Maxi was puzzled and lost for words, there was such a jumble in his head. In the end he stammered:

"The stupid bitch! Sisters, I tell you, she's nothing but trouble! But...! Jesus Christ!" Finally it occurred to him to ask: "Who is it?"

"Sir, he says he's the father of the girl who was killed here."

"Cynthia. Yeah. She was at school with my sister. Uh huh ... I see."

"But maybe he was lying. He seems more like a policeman to me."

Maxi took a deep breath and said:

"I'll take care of it. Don't you worry."

"Sir ..."

"You're right, if he saw me, he must be a policeman. Other people wouldn't notice."

"Yes they would! I see you myself ..."

"Me? Where?"

"Sir, all the time! When you get up in the morning, when you take a nap in the afternoon ..."

She couldn't say anything more because of the lump in her throat. Maxi, who thought she was speaking metaphorically, reassured her with his best smile. He didn't know what to say. She murmured something and walked off.

Maxi headed for home, exhausted, asleep on his feet. He had too much to think about, and it was all getting mixed up. Halfway back, he began to regret not having asked her more questions, some of which were blindingly obvious. For example, where she lived. Or her name. Although, of course, if he *did* know her from somewhere, those questions would have been tactless. But he might have asked about the garment she was carrying.... Could there be dry-cleaners in the heart of the shantytown? What if his wildest hunches turned out to be true? It didn't really matter: his questions could wait until the next time he saw her.

Suddenly he stopped as if a bolt of lightning had struck him on the head. Now he remembered where he knew her from! He couldn't believe it ... but it *was* her.... The memory had been triggered by thinking about her last words: "When you get up in the morning...." He'd seen her, he saw her every day, in the mirror that hung on the wall in front of his bed. A little black figure making meaningless gestures, who turned to face him from time to time. He could only see her from his bed, from a certain angle, and he had always supposed that it was some kind of flaw in the glass of the mirror, which happened to resemble a human silhouette an inch high. But no! It was her! The last person he would have expected to meet in reality. And he wasn't dreaming. He'd spoken to her, he'd touched her ... no, he hadn't actually touched her. But it wasn't a dream. She had come out of the mirror to warn him. She wanted to protect him....

Even if she was a magical being, she had given a very intense impression of reality. As well as being a mirror fairy, she was a flesh-and-blood girl: poor, not very pretty, and probably a servant (yes: she had mentioned her "employers"). He resolved to do something for her if he could. He'd show her there were still some good people. He wasn't sure how, but he'd think of something. He wouldn't rush; he'd let the situation itself indicate the action required. It wouldn't be like what he did for the collectors; it would be carefully considered, not improvised. That was the only way to return the favor. In fact, he already had an idea.

VI

THE IDEA HAD TAKEN A VERY VAGUE FORM IN HIS MIND, and in accordance with his determination not to improvise, he gave it time to mature. Meanwhile months went by. Winter passed. This was one of the happiest periods of Maxi's life, though he couldn't have said why. Perhaps because he felt that he had no obligations or plans, just a vague hope, within which something—he didn't know what—was slowly ripening.

Sometimes, when he woke up in the morning, he saw the little woman in black moving in the mirror facing his bed. Now that they had met and spoken, it was a delight to see her; she lit up his day. He thought he could make out the features of her face, a millimeter across at the most, and when she turned toward him, he waved. Dreamily, he even thought he could see her smiling at him with a "serious smile," although, on such a tiny scale, it was difficult to tell. Then during the day, when he remembered, he went to the mirror to look, but couldn't find her, even when he put his nose to the glass. "She's working now," he thought, "or she's gone home to the shantytown." Where could she be? What could she be doing? However long he peered, all he could see was his own face: the face of an overgrown child, with its clear, empty eyes. He hadn't seen her since that night, except there in the mirror.

One morning he woke up much earlier than usual. It was still dark. Light from the street lamps shone in through the window, and he heard the voices of the policemen changing shifts. All of a sudden he was completely awake and he had a strange feeling. He wondered if he'd been dreaming. That would have been unprecedented: he never dreamed, or always forgot his dreams completely. This time, in any case, he remembered nothing. He looked at the mirror but, of course, she wasn't there. It was too early; his friend was an effect of the daylight.

Then he decided to make the best of this brutally early start: he'd finally beat the hobo and catch him sleeping. Over the previous months, they had continued to run their motionless race: Maxi had never arrived early enough to see the boy asleep, and they still hadn't spoken or exchanged any kind of greeting. All they did was look at each other as Maxi went past. The winter had been very cold, and Maxi wondered anxiously how the poor boy could sleep out in the open like that. He tried to see how he'd managed, discreetly surveying the relics of the night. There were lots of newspapers; he must have wrapped himself in them; they were supposed to be good insulation. But even so...! Maxi never saw any blankets, and the boy was always wearing the same clothes. Luckily it hadn't rained.

At the onset of the cold weather, Maxi had resolved to stop and talk with the hobo one morning, on some pretext or other, or just like that. All he had to do was say, "Hi! I keep seeing you here. Don't you have a home? I've got some old clothes that might fit you. Shall I bring them tomorrow?" That was the idea: to give him clothes, woolen socks, for example. Later, he could do something else, maybe help him find a place to live. It was all a matter of breaking the ice, but Maxi kept putting it off, perhaps because he was shy, or afraid of offending or frightening the boy, who knows? In the end, he decided that he'd do it when he saw the boy asleep and not before. Now he realized that the challenge had been futile, like a race against the infinite, because the boy would have been woken by the cold in the small hours of the morning; he can't have been getting much sleep at all. And however early Maxi woke, he always stayed in bed to watch the animated figurine in the mirror. It was her fault that he never arrived in time.

But now the mirror was empty, and it was still dark outside. He leaped out of bed. Some association of ideas, favored by the unfamiliar hour, made him wonder if he'd been dreaming and, perhaps, still was. But the breakfast he bolted down was no dream, nor were the gym gear and the towel that he threw into his bag. He was already in the elevator, then down in the street. He started walking toward the freeway, in a hurry, very focused. But having reached the corner and waited for a car to pass, he was struck by a curious fact: however early you go out, you always see people who are out already. Besides, it wasn't as early as he'd thought. It was a trick of the light: the clouds that had filled the sky were casting their dark-gray shadows over the world.

Just after crossing the street he ran into his young friend from the mirror, rushing along, all dressed in black as usual, with her eyes half closed and an enigmatic expression on her face. Maxi froze in surprise and opened his arms:

"Hi!"

"Sir, hello …"

It was her! Or was it? Yes, it was; who else could it be? Out of context, he didn't recognize her. She had no distinctive features. And what was her context, anyway? The mirror? That was too unreal, and it made her look tiny, like a fly. The shantytown? But he'd only seen her there the once, and that was months ago, at night. Whatever the case, she had stopped in front of him because he was blocking her way.

"I didn't recognize you," he said. His vision was at its weakest in that night-like day. "It's not you," he hastened to explain, "it's my eyes."

"Sir, it's hard to see anything!"

"What? For you too?"

"Sir, I recognized you by your height, not your face."

In Maxi's bewilderment, a new world was beginning to open. Later in the day, he would take the time to develop that inkling and come to the conclusion that perhaps—this was a mere hypothesis, but a specially rich and promising one—perhaps it was true for everyone, not just him, that brighter light meant better vision. After all, that would be logical; he couldn't understand why it hadn't occurred to him before.

"I got up early today …"

"Sir, yes, I see."

He was going to say: "Today you won't be able to see me from the mirror in my room," but he didn't dare. He opted for something more ambiguous:

"You go to work so early!"

"Sir, that's how it is."

The conversation had played itself out, and with the subtlest hint of a smile, she signaled that she was about to continue on her way, as if he had been holding her up and she was going to be late. Which reminded him that he was losing time as well, and his thoughts returned to the hobo. That was when an idea that he had been vaguely toying with for ages finally crystallized, and, on an impulse, he decided that this was the perfect opportunity to put it into practice.

"You're in a such a hurry to go and get in the mirror! But there's something I want to tell you. When do you go home?"

"Sir, at half-past seven."

"Mmm ... that's a bit early. Are you busy at nine?"

"Sir, no."

"OK, listen. Tonight at nine, meet me at 1800 Bonorino, on the wide street there, you know where I mean?"

"Sir, yes."

"Make sure you're there, OK? Don't forget. I want to introduce you to someone."

And then, with a resonant "See you!" he walked on, finally. He went as fast as he could, almost running. He didn't want to be late, now that he'd committed himself. He was so preoccupied that he didn't notice anything on the way. He was thinking that his plan couldn't fail. If the hobo was awake, he'd talk to him anyway. It didn't even occur to Maxi that he might not be there. But, as it turned out, he wasn't. He was gone! Maxi froze, incredulous, staring at the place where, day after day, he'd seen the skinny figure of the hobo in his blue jacket and trousers, silhouetted against the wall. He couldn't believe his bad luck. The

boy was always there; he'd been there every day for months....
But not today! Today of all days!

Luckily, curiosity prompted him to do what he had never
done before: that is, to step through the weeds and venture into
that "private" space, the hobo's "bedroom." It was almost as if,
in the depths of his disappointment, he was identifying with
the boy, taking his place so that he would be "at home," even
though he was out. But it turned out that he *was* at home. Maxi
almost stood on him. His mistake was partly due to habit—he'd
been expecting to see an upright figure, as usual, and hadn't even
looked at the ground—but it was also caused in part by something that Maxi should have expected: the boy was very well hidden. He was lying in a dip, a sort of niche in the ground, and was
all covered in newspapers, even his head. Unless you were really
paying attention, it looked like any old heap of papers.

Maxi breathed a sigh of relief, as if all his problems were
solved. "That's lucky!" he thought. And it seemed an appropriate
thought because since he had taken to passing that way, he had
come to feel—without expressing it in so many words—that the
hobo was bringing him luck, which was why he was so punctual.
It would have been harder for Maxi to say why he needed luck
in the first place. Wasn't he lucky already? It was the others who
needed luck: the collectors, for example, or the people who lived
in the shantytown, or this homeless kid. But him? Why him? And
yet he too needed luck. In fact, that was the reason for everything
he did, all his strange and futile rites: they were meant "to bring
him luck." And in a way, they worked.

In that state of relief and release, Maxi felt as if time had
stopped, or as if he'd been chasing after time for an eternity and

had finally caught up. He put his bag down and sat on it, next to the sleeping boy.

Maxi couldn't see the boy's face, but it must have been him. He wasn't going to wake him up. Let him sleep a bit longer, poor kid. Why should he have to get up early, if he didn't have to go to work and there was no one expecting him? Let him enjoy the merciful oblivion of sleep for as long as he could. True, he was normally up by that time, but Maxi guessed that the cold of the early morning had been waking him (or maybe the fear of being discovered), so perhaps he had gone on sleeping for a change because the gathering storm had led to a rise in the temperature. Maxi, after rushing to get there, was covered in sweat. He sat still and kept perfectly quiet.

He admired the care that had gone into making the cocoon of newspaper, which enveloped the sleeper literally from head to foot. The boy must have had a lot of practice. Maxi could confirm that he had held out, in those conditions, night after night, all through that bitter winter. And now the winter was coming to an end. It was amazing how quickly it had gone by, he thought; almost like in a film, when there's a big gap in time between scenes, and the viewers have to use their imaginations to fill it in. But in this case it had been real time, and the boy had endured, with the mettle of an unknown hero. Maxi felt proud of him, perhaps because he identified the hobo with his own luck. What a brave kid! No one else he knew would have dared to do something like that and gone through with it, and so discreetly, too, with such humility. People with far less to brag about went around posing as heroes. It was an exclusive test, perhaps for just one person in the world. Gently, Maxi placed his hand on the

newspapers and felt the warmth coming from inside. He would
have to content himself with that sensation because it looked like
he wasn't going to see the boy asleep, in the end. Unless he lifted
one of the sheets very carefully, by a corner, and took a quick
peek. Why not? He rubbed his hands and flexed his fingers, like
a thief getting ready to crack a safe, or a card sharp about to go
for broke. Then he leaned forward stealthily.

The pages were from an old issue of *Clarín*, or two or three
different issues, because there were so many. As he looked for an
edge to peel back, a familiar name caught his eye: "Bonorino."
But that wasn't all; he noticed that the name was preceded by a
number that was also familiar: "1800." He had pronounced that
number and name himself just a few minutes earlier; he was so
thrown, he couldn't remember where or why, but those syllables were still ringing in his ears. Was it a coincidence? Or was it
magic? Intrigued, he began to read, which was unusual for him;
after the last set of exams in July he had thought that he would
never read anything again. And in fact, as this little exercise revealed, he was already forgetting how to do it. He made very slow
progress, deciphering word by word. But it wasn't just him: the
paper was dirty and faded, and the cocoon's uneven surface made
the lines twist and turn, so Maxi had to keep tilting his head to
follow them. Nevertheless, he got the gist. It was a letter of some
kind from the father of the girl who got killed in the neighborhood a while back, in summer or autumn. He knew about it because the girl, Cynthia, had been at school with his sister; and for
weeks it was all they could talk about at home. Echoes of the incident came back to him one by one, and, by a series of strange co-
incidences, resonated with the present situation. For a start, he'd

forgotten that Cynthia had lived at 1800 Bonorino and died there. But there was something else: Cynthia Cabezas was a poor girl, *shanty trash* as his sister put it (he'd never met her), the kind of girl who'd normally be working as a servant, not going to high school. Especially not an exclusive, super-expensive school like Misericordia. She had a scholarship; she was the "fly in the pail of milk," the odd one out. Maxi's sister and her friends hadn't excluded Cynthia, but only because discrimination was unfashionable, and they were slaves to fashion, especially Vanessa. All the same, he'd noticed the satisfaction in their voices when they talked about her mediocre grades, and the covertly festive fatalism with which they greeted her sad demise. What the crime had showed was that your origins always catch up with you in the end.

Anyway, that death, which was still unexplained, cast long shadows, and now Maxi remembered an argument that he'd had with Vanessa about it, when she had said that she was being followed by Cynthia's father ... the Ignacio Cabezas who had written the letter. Cabezas had also led a movement against the evangelical pastors who were recruiting in the shantytowns. In this he had been discreetly supported by the Catholic Church, and that was why the nuns at the Misericordia school had given his daughter a scholarship. But after the crime, a rumor went around that in fact he was working for a rival Protestant group, and then the sects began to accuse each other of being fronts for drug-dealing gangs. What Maxi found most surprising, when he came to the end of the letter, was the timing. Why, he wondered, was Cabezas writing to *Clarín* now? It didn't occur to him that the paper could be six months old. He didn't even know that newspapers had the date printed at the top of each page, so he didn't think to look. For Maxi, who had never read one in his life, every paper was "today's."

He emerged from this cogitation with a doubt. He knew what the letter was about and who had written it, but he still wasn't sure to whom it was addressed and why. He thought he must have missed something and was about to reread it, but when he looked down again what he saw, in the place where the letter had been, was a pair of eyes looking up at him.

He got such a fright he almost fell over backward. He didn't quite lose his balance, but he drew back abruptly and lifted his hand (rather than letting it hover idly, he put it to work scratching an ear) and curved his lips in an apologetic smile, all without taking his eyes off the hobo. With a great scrunching of papers, the white chrysalis came apart all at once.

"Did I frighten you?" asked Maxi. "I was waiting for you to wake up."

"Sir, good morning."

Oddly, the light had continued to dwindle instead of getting brighter; the clouds had darkened and descended so far it seemed you could reach out and touch them. Maxi's eyesight was functioning poorly in that gray dimness, but he was close enough to get a good view of the boy's face, which, he now realized, he had never actually seen before. He had recognized him by his silhouette, in the context of a particular place and time, and had he seen him somewhere else, in different clothes, he could easily have taken him for a complete stranger. Maxi was shocked by what he saw. The boy had come through the difficult trial of winter, but what a price he'd paid! His face was gaunt, dirty and drawn, his hair all stuck together, and if not for the gleam of hunger and anxiety in his eyes, they might have belonged to a corpse. Luckily he had no facial hair. It occurred to Maxi that, for once, he'd arrived just in time.

That was why he decided not to beat around the bush but to get straight to the point. Anyway, it was better to start with something practical and concrete rather than trying to strike up a conversation because he wouldn't have known what to say:

"There's this place I'm going to tell you about. Be there at nine tonight, and I'll introduce you to someone."

The hobo nodded seriously and waited. Maxi's mind was a blank; he didn't know how to continue.

"Sir, what place?"

"Oh, yes." He giggled. "What a dope. I tell you to go there but I don't say where it is." He looked around, trying to orient himself, with some difficulty. In the end he pointed in a direction, more or less at random. "1800 Calle Bonorino. It's a street that widens out. There's a vacant lot and a big empty space ..."

"Sir, yes, I know."

"OK, that's where, at nine. Do you want me to lend you my watch?"

The hobo glanced at Maxi's Rolex and shook his head energetically.

"Sir, no, I'll ask."

"OK then."

"Sir, is it for a job?"

The question took Maxi by surprise. He dodged it with a prevarication:

"Something like that. But better. You'll see."

And off he went. He continued to the gym on autopilot, think-ing about what he'd done. And what he hadn't done: like giving the boy a few pesos for something to eat, or saying something more enticing about the appointment to make sure he'd turn up.... But he didn't know what he could have said, and maybe it was best to stick to the minimum; for someone who had so little, the minimum was probably enough. And Maxi had only a vague idea of what was going to happen. He would introduce them: the hobo and the mirror-girl, his two best friends.... He felt that they were made for each other, they were complemen-tary; together they could make their way in the world. Each had what the other lacked. She had a job, a home; she could give him shelter. He had the courage and the experience that she needed to emerge from the mirror's ethereal waters and the dark heart of the shantytown, and take her place in reality. There was no pre-dicting what would happen later on, but they might fall in love, why not? Anything was possible.

Maxi rushed on, blind and deaf to his surroundings, com-pletely absorbed in his thoughts. No one noticed him because all the people who crossed his path were in a hurry too, rushing to beat the storm, which looked as though it was about to break.

He was walking on air. He couldn't believe it had all worked out so easily; he didn't stop to think that, in fact, nothing at all had worked out yet. But results were secondary. The masterpiece came first. In the end, after all the time he'd spent thinking about it (or not: it came to the same thing), the operation had per-formed itself; he'd barely had to intervene. After all that thinking, and promising not to let what he did be governed by impulse or circumstances, it had been an improvisation on the spur of the moment. That's why it had been easy; that's why it had seemed to happen all by itself.

And yet Maxi felt that what he had done had grown out of the most patient and careful deliberation. Even though he had improvised.

Either this was a contradiction or the term "improvisation" would have to be redefined. People always assume that to improvise is to act without thinking. But if you do something on an impulse, or because you feel like it, or just like that, without knowing why, it's still *you* doing it, and you have a history that has led to that particular point in your life, so it's not really a thoughtless act, far from it; you couldn't have given it any more thought: you've been thinking it out ever since you were born.

VII

MAYBE IT WAS STILL VERY EARLY — WITH ALL THE BACK
and forth between "early" and "late" Maxi had lost track of the
time—or maybe it was because of the storm; in any case, when
he got to the gym, it was empty. He wasn't surprised; he was usually the first to arrive. The members started turning up around
eight-thirty, and the instructors and receptionists came at nine.
Saturno, the man who worked at the bar and usually opened up,
was nowhere to be seen. Still, he must have come, because the
place was open and the lights were on. Maxi guessed that he'd
gone out, as usual, to buy fruit for juicing and milk and crois-
sants.... He must have been a very early riser because Maxi had
never beaten him to the gym. And there was another minor or
maybe not-so-minor mystery that Maxi had never been able to
fathom. Each morning when he arrived, the cleaning was already
done; the place had been swept and mopped and tidied up. He
would have assumed that it was done at night, after closing time,
except that when he got there, first thing in the morning, the
dressing-room floor was still wet from being mopped. And he
was sure that Saturno was the one who opened up. That's what
he'd heard people say. But his puzzlement never lasted longer

than the few minutes it took him to change and begin his exercise routine; once he was pumping, he thought about nothing else.

So he went into the gym and headed for the dressing room, but as he was walking past the little curved bar, something behind it caught his eye. It was Saturno, lying on the floor. Maxi dropped his bag and kneeled beside him, unsure what to do. The recumbent body was not quite still, indicating that Saturno was, at least, alive. "Don't move him," Maxi thought, remembering instructions that he had once heard; but he also remembered that those instructions applied to people injured in accidents, which didn't seem to be the case here. Anyhow, he had to call an ambulance.

Looking more closely, he realized that the movement he had noticed was concentrated in Saturno's lips: he must have been trying to speak. His eyes were closed. Maxi bent down but still couldn't hear anything. Maybe the movements were twitches or spasms. Even so, he wanted to be sure, so he bent further down, turned his head and put his ear to the mouth of the fallen man. Then he did hear something: a few words or phrases that seemed very clear and distinct, but so faint that only someone with auditory superpowers could have understood them. It was like what happens when you have the impression that a switched-off radio is still transmitting, but even if you put your ear right up against the speaker, you can't hear a thing. Luckily, the gym was absolutely quiet, otherwise Maxi's experiment would have failed straight away. He concentrated as hard as he could. Finally he recognized or thought he recognized a word:

"... Maxi ..."

He recoiled and looked at Saturno in amazement. The bar-man's face was still inert, except for the twitching of his lips. Maxi lowered his ear again, and resumed his concentration.

". . . don't be scared, it's nothing. It's my heart again. Sit me up."

"What?" He had meant to whisper, but it came out as a shout because he couldn't control his thundering voice.

"Are you deaf or just pretending? Sit me up, I said."

Maxi was so stunned he couldn't react. A dialogue was pos-sible, it seemed, but it was a dialogue with a dead man, whose voice was separated from his body. This impression was rein-forced by the nature of Saturno's command, because Maxi had always heard the verb "to sit" used intransitively, referring to a position that you adopt for yourself—"I sit," "you sit," "he sits"—and this "sit *me* up" sounded like an impossible cross be-tween the first and second persons. In spite of which, he under-stood. But in order to understand he had to imagine the person who had spoken as dead and yet react as if he were alive. This reminded him of something that often happened at home. When his parents were watching TV chat shows with showbiz person-alities, and some old actor came on, they would always say: I thought he was dead! Me too! I could have sworn he died ages ago! And even though the actor would be talking about his cur-rent work and projects for the future, they kept seeing him as a dead man, at once historical and forgotten, a ghost from their childhood or further back still, from the age of silent cinema or the traveling theaters of the nineteenth century. Maxi had no idea who these actors were, but he would get caught up in the parental reminiscing, and in the end they came to seem familiar.

He kept his ear to Saturno's mouth. Not because he wasn't convinced, but because he'd begun to enjoy it. But if he had to sit him up, that was what he had to do. The logical solution would have been to sit him on the floor and prop his back against the fridge; as well as being easy to do, it would have left him in a comfortable position. But Maxi didn't think of that. Instead, he lifted Saturno up and sat him on the high stool behind the bar. His legs dangled, and since the stool had no back, Maxi had to keep hold of him. The barman's body felt as heavy as a mass of solid lead. Maxi took Saturno's hands and placed them on the bar, like a pianist's hands on a keyboard.

"Shall I call an ambulance?"

He put his ear to Saturno's mouth again. It was more awkward now.

"No, leave me like this. I'll be right in a minute."

Maxi tried letting him go, to see if he was stable. He had to shift him a few inches so that his center of gravity was in line with the middle of the stool, but then he stayed put. His eyes were still closed.

"I'll get changed and come straight back," Maxi said.

He picked up his bag and headed for the dressing room, but before going through the door, he turned to take a last look at Saturno. The bartender was still there, in exactly the same position, with his eyes closed. He looked very fragile, perched on that high stool, and was liable, Maxi had to admit, to fall at any moment. Saturno was a middle-aged man. Not old—he wouldn't have been sixty—but jaded, worn down by a routine job and a pessimistic character. His life had not been happy. Starved of love, his heart was rebelling against its owner.

There are so many people like that! thought Maxi. Life feeds on life, it has no choice. Life stokes its furnace with life, but not with life in general; it burns the unique and particular life of the individual, and when there's nothing left to feed to the flames, the fire goes out. And yet ... no one is alone in this. There are others, many, many others, each living his life or hers, and on it goes. The little voice that he had heard, so distant or rather ... so tiny—a miniature voice, a dollhouse voice, to be studied under a microscope—that little voice was conveying a message from another dimension. An echo, miniaturized by distance, but a distance that was neither spatial nor temporal. And yet that miniature interval could make all the difference in the world, as when a minute's delay prevents an encounter that might have changed the course of a life.... In fact, thought Maxi, a marginal shift with respect to the time or the space of others—a minute, a second, a inch—could mean that you end up living in a different reality, where any kind of magic might be possible.

When he walked into the dressing room he was always a little surprised to see the floor still wet from being mopped, but this morning there was something far more surprising than water on the floor: the semi-naked body of a young woman, lying as if she'd been suddenly struck down. She was bathed in the light shining in through the sliding doors that opened onto the balcony, which the sheen of the wet tiles intensified. The warmth of her body had evaporated some of the floor's moisture, creating a kind of vaporous aureole around her.

It was such a surprise that Maxi stopped dead with his head tilted slightly forward. He forgot about the swinging door, which he had shoved open, so when it came swinging back, and his hand wasn't there to stop it, the wood struck him on the forehead with a resonant *clunk* that echoed all through the gym. Maxi staggered backward, recoiling from the blow, and for a moment his vision went blank. When the world reappeared, the door was shut in front of him. He opened it again, keeping hold of it this time, and slipped inside. What he had seen before was still there, exactly the same. He approached the girl, rubbing his forehead, where a bump had started to form.

When he was standing over her, Maxi realized who she was: Jessica, one of the morning regulars, and one of the earliest starters, though not as early as him. It was strange that he hadn't recognized her before, since he saw her every day. But when it comes to recognizing people, he thought, it all depends on context, and he had always seen Jessica in her leotard, working out on one of the machines, chatting and laughing: nothing like this lifeless figure, and yet it was her.

The first thing that occurred to Maxi was that she had slipped on the wet floor. Except that there were no footprints; it was almost as if the floor had been mopped around her. He turned around and saw that his own footprints were clearly visible.

He knelt down to examine her—this was becoming a habit. Jessica was breathing deeply and gently, as if asleep. Maxi looked at her lips: they were slightly open, pink and motionless. With her, getting up close to listen would have been more pleasant, and suddenly he found himself wondering dreamily what she would say to him, what her "little voice" would sound like.... She was beautiful, she really was beautiful, a dream come true.... How odd that he hadn't noticed before, although he saw her every day. But that must depend on the context as well, he thought. In the end, sleep and waking were the fundamental pair of contexts from which all the others were derived. A pair of words came to mind: "sleeping beauty." Maybe she was one of those girls who's always tense when she's awake, and can only relax and allow her beauty to blossom when she falls asleep. The naked pink of her eyelids and lips continued under the folds of the only garment she was wearing: a white T-shirt of lightweight fabric. Her breasts were just visible, pink and white. She wasn't wearing underwear: the mishap must have caught her by surprise while she was getting changed. But Maxi looked around and couldn't see clothes or a bag or anything. And besides, it was the men's dressing room: she wouldn't have come in here to get changed.

In the absence of instructions to follow, Maxi felt he had to do something: get her off that cold, wet floor, for example, and lay her on one of the one of the long wooden benches. Which he did, rather slowly, on the pretext of being careful, but really to savor the experience of holding her in his arms. Once on the bench, she sighed and seemed to be on the point of waking. Since her T-shirt had ridden up during the maneuver, leaving her visible up to the waist, Maxi felt embarrassed and afraid that he'd have to explain himself, so he looked around again for clothes or anything, a stray towel, say, with which to cover her up. And then he saw that there was a bag, in full view, sitting on the other bench, a big gym bag. How could he have missed it before? He crossed the room with two strides, looked for the zipper, and before opening the bag, glanced back at Jessica. She was still asleep. He unzipped the bag and rummaged around inside. How strange. It contained men's clothes: shorts, a tracksuit, a singlet, a pair of enormous shoes (she had little pink doll's feet) and even men's deodorant and shampoo, the same brand he used. . . . Everything in the bag looked familiar, but he still hadn't realized why: it was his bag; he had left it there when he came in, before kneeling down. This absurd befuddlement could only be explained by his agitation and, perhaps, the blow to his head. Neither of which prevented Maxi from momentarily envisaging the strange possibility that the bag concealed a secret: maybe Jessica was in fact a man, or a man was impersonating her, or something like that.

The mistake did have one benefit, though: it proved that he wasn't thinking straight, that he was losing the plot. He should have been trying to revive her or help her somehow, instead of imagining nonsense. So he went and sat down next to her, put his hand under the nape of her neck, and lifted her head. Her hair was so silky, so fine!

Jessica opened her eyes . . . they were eyes that Maxi had never really seen: large and dark, with streaks of gold that made them very still, veiled now with silence and bewilderment. He let himself sink into them, quiet like her, enfolded in a dream. But he snapped out of it when he heard her say his name:

"Maxi. . . !"

She sounded surprised, as if he were the last person she was expecting to see at that moment.

"Jessica! What happened? Are you OK? Did you faint?"

"Uh? What?" She moved her head, which was still cradled in his hand, but didn't sit up. Her confusion settled into a little smile. "I fainted, or I fell asleep. I don't know . . ."

"You were lying on the floor!"

"I think my blood pressure dropped. I shouldn't have got up so early.... It's the weather, the storm."

"I think the sun's come out now."

"What do you mean? The sky's about to fall! You never notice what's happening around you."

"No, I think ..."

They both looked at the glass doors to the balcony, which were painted green except for a strip at the top. A dark gray, almost nocturnal light was coming in through that strip. The silence was supernatural, as if the world really was about to end. Maxi let his gaze stray to the mirror that covered one of the walls and saw himself there, like the Virgin in a Pietà, holding in his arms that warm, pink object: a woman. They seemed to be floating in a greenish element. Then he remembered:

"The same thing happened to Saturno. I left him to recover."

"Really? Him too? Then ..."

"It must be the weather."

"Yeah ... it must be. Him too?"

"He was lying on the floor like you."

Maxi nearly added, "Although he was dressed," but he stopped himself in time and said: "He didn't want me to call an ambulance."

"No!" she exclaimed with a shudder. "There's no need, not for me, anyway. I'm fine now." She put her hands on the bench to sit up, but then changed her mind, as if reluctant to abandon the comfort of Maxi's arms. "Give me a minute."

"There's no hurry." They remained silent for a moment. "But how come you were in the men's dressing room?"

She looked at him, puzzled.

"What do you mean?" she eventually asked. "There's a men's dressing room and a women's dressing room?"

"Yes … I think so. I always get changed here."

"Me too. Is there another one?"

Maxi thought about it.

"You know, I've never checked. I come really early, you see, and there's never anyone else around …"

She shook her head wearily.

"No, Maxi, it's not that. It's because you don't notice … you live in your own private world."

"I don't think I'm really that bad. Anyway, even if you're right, I'm not hurting anyone; the opposite, in fact!" After all, it was the second time that morning that he'd come to the aid of someone who had fainted.

"Yes you are, Maxi. You have victims whether you know it or not. You walk right past, you don't even see us."

"I saw you. If it was like you say, I would have stepped over your body, got changed and gone to work out, leaving you there on the floor."

She didn't answer. She had been distracted, not by something else but by him. She was staring.

"What happened to your forehead?"

Maxi touched it.

"I hit it on the door."

"You've got a huge bump. The door? Did you think you could walk through it, like a ghost?"

Before he could answer, he saw a grimace distort her beautiful face, and she cried out.

"Agghh! Maxi!"

"What is it? What?"

"I've lived through this already. It's an exact repetition! Absolutely exact, down to the last detail!"

"Including the bump?"

"Don't make fun of me. It's amazing! It's a déjà-vu. Including the fact that I know it's a déjà-vu ..."

"When you remember that the other time you thought it was a déjà-vu too, that means it's over."

"But I'm not sure it's over this time. It's like it's still going on, more faintly, or differently.... It's beautiful but it's horrible too."

"It makes sense that it's two things at once because it's a double experience."

"You know why it happened? Because I was thinking of you when I fainted, and when I came to, the first thing I saw was your face."

As an explanation it was dubious, but he felt flattered anyway. Who doesn't like to be the object of other people's thoughts?

"Thank you very much."

"What for?"

"For thinking of me." He blushed.

"You're blushing. Your whole face has gone the color of your bump. You're so shy, such a little boy. That's why all the women are in love with you."

"You're exaggerating."

"Don't go so red, please! You look like a chili."

He giggled uncomfortably.

"I can't help it."

"It's all part of the same thing. A little boy has no idea what's going on around him. No one has any reason to thank him because he never wastes a second of his time thinking about other people."

"Jessica, I'm sorry, but I think you're contradicting yourself. Either you think about other people, or you pay attention to your surroundings. You can't do both at the same time."

"That's so typical of you, to make that distinction. As if we weren't surrounded by other people. You're just proving me right."

Maxi wasn't sure how they had reached these bewildering dialectical heights, so he simply replied with a smile. He could feel his forehead throbbing, with an almost audible beat. Jessica half closed her eyes and went on, contradicting her own contradictions:

"What you have to realize is you're not the only one. It happens to us all. Not so much with people, because they find ways to grab our attention and occupy our thoughts, so we keep tabs on them. But with things and places. It's like living in a labyrinth that's always being modified. It's amazing how much you can end up not knowing. Everything."

"I get by OK."

She continued with her train of thought:

"Have you noticed how some people are always doing home renovations and are never satisfied? God's like that too. With humans it's so common that the council has to hire planes to take aerial photos. That way they can see the renovations and adjust the rates accordingly."

"Are you serious?" asked Maxi.

"And that's nothing. If they want, they can reconstruct all your movements, everything you did in the course of a day, everything you said, what people said to you ... everything."

"No, I think you're exaggerating."

"I'm not, Maxi, you're so naïve! You're such a daydreamer!"

"Who'd be interested in what I do?"

"You never know. Anything at all can turn out to be important."

Maxi pondered this:

"Anyway, when you're inside, they can't see you."

"What do you mean? No, you didn't understand. I wasn't talking about the planes. There's a thousand ways to document all the stuff that happens. Everything gets recorded somehow."

"Hmm ... yeah, maybe. With hidden microphones or cameras."

"No. It was the same before they were invented. But now there are cameras as well, even here ..."

Maxi laughed:

"Don't be paranoid. Who's going to put a camera in a gym?"

"I wouldn't be at all surprised. And even without a camera, I'm sure that ..."

Was Maxi imagining it or were tears beginning to well in the big golden eyes gazing up at him? He was embarrassed and didn't know what to say. She went on:

"Now that the gym's closing, somebody might want to know everything that's happened here, minute by minute, since it opened. It might be important, for some reason. And there are so many traces! If you really think about it, everything you've done has left some kind of mark. Someone remembers it. Even when you're alone, it's like you're being watched, because there's always someone who can calculate or deduce what you're doing. All they have to do is gather the data and sort it out ..."

"Hang on a minute," said Maxi, who hadn't been keeping up. "Why did you say the gym's closing? Was that hypothetical?"

"What? Don't you know? Come on...! See how right I was before when I said you go round with your head in the clouds? Of course it's closing. Chin Fu was just renting, and now the owner wants the premises back. He has heaps of places, all over Buenos Aires, and he's leasing them out to an evangelical church so they can be used for services. He's kicking out all the old tenants, refusing to renew their contracts. Either the church pays more or there's something else in it for him. You really didn't know?"

"No, truly. And when...?"

"Now! The gym might be history already. Didn't you notice that no one's here today?"

"Yes, but isn't that because it's so early?"

"It's not so early anymore. I was asleep for hours. Élida's not coming. We said goodbye yesterday."

Élida was the receptionist who worked there in the morning, a very nice lady.

"I had no idea."

"It all began when Cynthia died ..." said Jessica, but she stopped when she noticed that Maxi wasn't listening.

In an almost telepathic way, they had become simultaneously aware of the picture they composed together. They looked at the mirror-wall. Jessica couldn't help noticing that she was almost naked—her skin a pale glow in the midst of the shadowy gray-green splendor—and that she was lying in the arms of a young giant wrapped in a plastic raincoat. But she made no attempt to cover herself or move away. Circumstances, which might have arranged them in any number of ways, had placed them in precisely that position. The slightest variation in the events leading up to that moment would have produced a different result. Yet this was how it had turned out. It was as if the hero of a fable, who had set out to rescue a princess, had, in the course of his marvelous adventures, been wounded on the sea shore, and a drop of his blood, carried by a wave, had voyaged to the far depths of the ocean and slipped in through the half-open jaws of an oyster to produce the rarest and most beautiful gem in the world: the pink pearl.

Now they were looking at each other. Maxi and Jessica. Her and him. Maxi was shy. Who isn't, deep down? Who hasn't succumbed to a despair more powerful than all the strength one might possibly muster, wondering how many first steps will have to be taken, how many actions performed and words spoken, how many labyrinths will have to be negotiated in order, finally, to reach the moment at which reality begins to happen. But when that moment comes, none of us are shy; we couldn't be, even if we tried. Things were happening to him now. He leaned down as the sky leans over the earth and kissed her. Lips touched lips that it had seemed they could never hope to touch, and that was all it took for their bodies and souls to communicate. If the gym no longer existed, everything was allowed. Trembling and enraptured, Jessica just had time to think, as if from far away: "He didn't ask anything, he didn't say anything. All he did was kiss me." And before she put her arms around him and shut her eyes, she came to this conclusion: "He's so clever."

VIII

ALL DAY THE STORM REMAINED IMMINENT, BUILDING steadily; the sky grew darker hour by hour, the temperature rose, the air thickened. At dusk, Maxi woke from the deep sleep of his siesta into a crepuscular limbo traversed by people making furtive dashes for the safety of their homes.

When his mother, who was working in the dining room, saw him heading for the door, she said, "Don't go far; it's going to start pouring any minute." She taught crafts in a high school, and was making complicated paper cut-outs. Maxi came to the table and picked one up, to be polite.

"That's pretty. What is it?" He turned it over and answered his own question: "A mushroom. A duster."

"A fan," said his mother. In fact it was a cluster of fans with a single handle, which opened out in turn to make another cluster, upside down. "A fan that fans itself."

"And you get your students to make these?" asked Maxi, intrigued by the artifact.

"It's an advanced class. But yes, they have to 'get it out.' Otherwise they fail."

"It must be hard for them," said Maxi, before adding ironically:

"But you're right to be tough; they need skills to equip them for life."

His mother just smiled. It was a topic they often debated: the usefulness of what she taught. He was amusing himself with the cut-out, opening and closing the fans.

"It's pretty. I like it."

"Can you leave it alone, Maxi? You're going to wreck it. One little twist and it's ruined for good. They can't be fixed, these things."

He put it down on the table, suspecting (with good reason) that the damage was already done.

"Do you still have to keep practicing? Don't you know it off by heart?"

"I'm always inventing something new. Sometimes I don't even know myself what it will turn out to be."

"You must have folded so many sheets of paper, Mom. It's amazing you don't have calluses on your fingers."

With that, he left. He headed for Rivadavia and crossed it, as usual. The weather was threatening, and people were in a hurry. Two or three times he emerged from his daydreams, thinking that it had begun to rain, but it was a false alarm each time. "If it starts, I'll go back home when I get to Bonifacio," he thought, before remembering that he had an appointment or, rather, two. He shook his head, smiling indulgently at himself: "What can you do? Head in the clouds." But then he saw the hitch. The rain could spoil everything. He shrugged his shoulders.

It didn't matter! What he had planned was beyond those contingencies. Anyway, he wasn't afraid of the rain ... or was he? He couldn't actually remember. He couldn't remember a time when it had rained. It's true that he was constantly distracted by one preoccupation or another, but it was still odd that he couldn't recall a single experience of rain. And yet he knew perfectly well what rain was. "And if I don't, I'm about to find out," he thought. He did have some excuse, however: it hadn't rained in Buenos Aires for months. And when a kind of weather isn't happening, we tend to forget what it's like.

In the vacant lots beside the railway he found someone who needed his help. But it was such an unusual day and he was so absorbed in his thoughts that he almost kept on walking. It was a woman, with a two- or three-year-old child; she was looking through the bags of trash and pushing a supermarket trolley. He stopped abruptly when he'd already passed her, and turned around. In general he didn't offer to help women on their own, for fear that that it might be taken the wrong way. But his fame must have spread among the collectors in the neighborhood, because it seemed that none of them could take it the wrong way now. Fame is always based on some kind of misunderstanding, but misunderstanding is everywhere: nothing is more universal. In any case, the woman was very mannish; her body, draped in an oversize nylon jacket, betrayed no signs of femininity. She was small and nervous, no doubt undernourished, with disheveled hair spilling out from under a woolen cap. Maxi took charge of the vehicle, and she seized the opportunity to speed up her rummaging, almost oblivious to the little girl, who trotted about on her own, until Maxi hoisted her into the trolley.

They headed west for a while until they got to the square, where the woman slipped in through the service entrance of a restaurant after dismissing her "draught horse," with whom she had exchanged no more than a few indistinct syllables. Perhaps because of the weather, she was in a hurry, on edge, like the two little guys with their super-size cart who were next in line for Maxi's help, and the family after that, with whom he crossed back over Rivadavia. The little guys specialized in cardboard, and had gathered a huge amount of it. Maxi liked to feel the weight of a really heavy load: it meant money for them, a good day's trading, although they'd never make a fortune. He loved to feel the transformation of such a light material into a serious weight, as the boxes piled up to form a mass.

What he didn't know was that, from a certain point on, two pairs of eyes had been watching him. They belonged to two girls: his sister, Vanessa, and her inseparable friend, Jessica, who were half a block behind, not letting him out of their sight. They had planned this operation carefully and decided to go through with it, in spite of the impending storm. They were determined to follow him all the way, and find out just what was going on; and the pursuit was meant to end with a confrontation in which they would lay all their cards on the table. They couldn't, or wouldn't, wait any longer: the time had come to enlist Maxi in the battle against the dark forces that were threatening them.

It was a task that required superhuman patience. The forward movement of their target was painfully slow and subject to all sorts of interruptions. They pretended to be looking in storefronts, or hid in doorways, or even turned around and went for a little walk to the corner and back. They weren't afraid that Maxi would notice them because he was so vague, and he'd never guess they were on his tail. But they couldn't lose sight of him or let him get too far away: they'd already seen how erratic his route was, and how he went from one scavenger to another without any warning or anything, just like that.

To pass the time, they chatted. That was nothing new: the substance of their friendship was endless conversation. They wouldn't have been able to explain how they kept coming up with topics but they never ran out. It was one of the reasons why they always made up after their frequent quarrels: their tongues missed the exercise, and with their other friends, there wasn't the same continuous flow. In fact, one of the richest topics or sets of topics was what had happened to them during the intervals when they hadn't been speaking to each other. Which was a reason to multiply those intervals, and now the fights were almost superfluous: all they needed to accumulate material was an instant, the tiniest gap.

On this occasion, there was no shortage of topics. They had been in a flurry putting their plan into action, so there were some really important stories still waiting to be told, and now, with Maxi and his damn scavengers stopping and starting all the time, they had an opportunity to catch up.

"This morning," said Jessica, "I ran into him at the gym and I realized something. You're not going to believe this—I didn't— but your brother hasn't realized that I'm me. He's an alien."

"He doesn't know that you...? I don't understand."

"He hasn't realized that the 'Jessica' he knows from the gym is the same 'Jessica' who's friends with his sister. For him, they're, I mean we're, two different people."

"No way. That is com-*plete*-ly ..." Vanessa was left gaping and gazing off into space, with the expression of someone who has just been apprised of an amazing fact and must hurriedly reorganize everything she knows to make a place for it.

Jessica knew exactly how she felt.

"I've been trying to work it out all day, and in the end I realized it's actually not impossible. I don't go to your place very often, and usually he's not there, and when he is, he doesn't pay attention to me. He's been ignoring his little sister's friends ever since he was a kid; they've become invisible to him. And when I call on the phone and he answers, I'm just a voice: 'Jessica,' his sister's friend. He puts you on and forgets all about it. It's not like the name's going to give it away; there are so many Jessicas. For him, the gym must be a world apart, separate from everything else, especially from you."

"And you never said anything?"

"Well, we've never talked much. Once he gets going on the machines, it's like other people don't exist. Today was the first time we really talked, and only because I had an accident."

"So did you tell him?"

Jessica hesitated for a moment:

"Listen, this is going to sound crazy, but it was only thinking about it later that I realized. And I don't know if I would have told him anyway: it would spoil the fun, don't you think? It's like having a secret identity, without all the bother of having to lie."

They took a few steps in silence. Maxi's cart had turned the corner; they crossed to the opposite sidewalk to keep their distance and avoid running into him in case he hadn't gone far. But no: he was thirty yards away, standing still, while a bunch of ragged children rushed around opening up bags of trash as quickly as they could. The girls pretended to be looking in the window of a hairdressing salon. Something had been bothering Vanessa:

"Why do you say you don't come to my place very often? We're together all day long!"

"Because it's true. Haven't you noticed how we hardly ever go to each other's places? I think it's because we live so close."

"And what about when you sleep over?"

"Well, OK, yeah ... it *is* kind of hard to believe, but that's what he's like, your brother."

"And what about when you went into his room?"

Jessica laughed. The incident, caused by a combination of sleepwalking and hallucination, had kept them up laughing all night at the time.

"He was asleep, and he didn't wake up."

"Just as well!"

They laughed again. Jessica had forgotten that episode, and remembering it now only added to the magic of the whole misapprehension. It made her realize how close she had been to Maxi, how they had shared a kind of intimacy, and yet she had remained a stranger to him. Vanessa's thoughts had gone in another direction:

"Maybe he was pulling your leg?"

"No, because we didn't talk about that. I'm sure, Vanessa."

"Are you going to say something?"

"Huh?"

"Are you going to say something, tomorrow, or the day after, at the gym?"

It took Jessica a moment to understand, and when she did, she was still surprised.

"Say something? Tell him that it's me? I don't know ... I don't know if there's anything to say.... And anyway, we're going to confront him tonight, aren't we? Isn't that what we agreed?"

"Yeah, that's right. He'll realize, when he sees you. Or maybe not."

Jessica remembered something and gave a start:

"But the gym's finished, Vanessa! Didn't I tell you? Chin Fu is closed, for good."

"Really?" said her friend, with a show of indifference, which was also largely genuine. She regarded going to the gym as ridiculous and unhealthy, a waste of time. It was a reaction against her brother, but also, perhaps, a sincere conviction on her part. Months back, when Jessica had joined up, Vanessa had explained exactly why it was a dumb idea, and there had even been a brief cooling of their friendship as a result. After that, Vanessa had made a point of never asking about the exercise program, and if Jessica brought it up, she pretended not to have heard or talked about something else. Now, watching Maxi, who had set off again, she said absently: "Good. Maybe they'll find something better to do with their time."

"But it's not like every gym in Buenos Aires is going to close, Vanessa! There are millions ..."

"Ugh."

"Though actually ... it's not the only one that's closing. That's something else we have to talk about with Maxi tonight."

"Why? What's he got to do with it?"

"I don't really know how this happened, but it's another indirect result of Cynthia's death. You remember her father was involved with those evangelical sects and their business deals? Well, after the crime, which they exploited to the hilt, their financial backer started kicking out all the gyms that used to rent spaces from him, and turning them into churches. And now he's gone and done it to Chin Fu, one of the last ones left in the neighborhood."

"How did they exploit Cynthia's death? I had no idea."

"They turned her into a saint! They pray to her, they ask her for help.... Didn't you know?"

"Are you serious? Like with Gilda?"

"Exactly!"

"They're crazy!"

They laughed. But something was still bothering Vanessa. They had walked on, following Maxi, and now they were in the middle of a dark block. Because of the stopping and starting and their vacillating attention, it was one of those erratic conversations: they kept leaving loose ends and then, all of a sudden, going back to pick them up.

"What accident?"

"Huh?"

"You said you talked to Maxi in the gym today because of an accident? Did you twist your wrist, or get a weight caught on your nipple or something?" Vanessa inquired venomously.

But the sarcasm was lost on Jessica, who, as soon as she remembered the morning's events, launched enthusiastically into the story:

"You'll never guess what happened to me. I almost died! What a dickhead! You know I've been buying proxidine from Saturno, the guy who works at the bar. With the gym closing down it was getting complicated, so he asked me to go there first thing, before anyone else turned up. So I go there really early this morning, and would you believe it, the son of a bitch gives me bad proxidine..."

Vanessa reacted with a horrified grimace.

"How do you mean bad? Fake?"

"How do I know? I wish it had just been fake. It had the opposite effect... I don't know... I began to feel like everything was getting further away instead of coming closer.... It was like the end of the world, or falling down a well. I fainted and when I came to, your brother was there."

"What a fuck-up! What did you say to him?"

"Nothing. That my blood pressure had dropped. But it's not Saturno's fault; they sold him bad stuff. I know because he took some, and it had the same effect on him, or worse: it messed with his heart. It must have something to do with all these changes: he buys from that guy they call the Pastor, who works as an informer for the sect that's going to take over the place. Later on he swapped what he'd sold me for some good stuff that he had from before."

Vanessa's interest, which had been flagging over the previous minutes, picked up suddenly.

"Have you got some here?"

"Of course." She put her hand in her pocket.

"Are you sure it's the good stuff?"

"Don't worry. I've tried it."

They looked in Maxi's direction to check that he wasn't going to get away from them, saw that he was standing still, and ducked into a doorway.

"Now they're getting high, the little whores," said Cabezas to himself in the darkness of his car, from which he had been observing their every move. Not to be outdone, he reached into his pocket and took out his own supply of proxidine. He kept it in a small red crystal flask, the size of an egg, which felt very hot. And it wasn't just a feeling: inside the crystal, the drug was in a gel solution, which, so he had been told, increased the proximity of the atoms, generating real heat. On the underside of the flask was a gold-plated spring-release mechanism, as on a lighter, which flicked out a needle a quarter-inch long. He pressed the needle into the lobe of his ear, frowning slightly as he felt the prick, and left it there for a few seconds, allowing the drug to penetrate. By a strange coincidence, just at that moment a wild bolt of lightning ripped across the sky, from one side of the windshield to the other, like a camera flash lighting up the policeman's bloated face, his dazed expression, and the crystal attached to his ear like a carnation of phosphorescent fire.

Ecstasy enveloped him from within. He needed that, and much more besides. His old problems had intensified and were building to a crisis. His nemesis, the judge who had sworn to destroy him, was hot on his heels, accumulating evidence, and no doubt preparing her final attack. But he would be a step ahead ... thanks to that pair of teenagers, the not-so-innocent pawns in his Machiavellian plan.

At the age of fifty, ravaged by failure, by the slow, corrosive contamination of crime, by divorce and fatigue, just when there seemed to be nothing left for him ... Cabezas had discovered that he still had time; and in the time that he had left, whether it was long or short, he could do a lot. But not a lot of anything. That was precisely what was ending or had already come to an end: the free, open possibility of anything. There was one path left, and only one: evil. That was the way to renewal and action. He had discovered that he wasn't too old for that. When every other avenue was closed to him, when it was all definitively finished ... a path opened up in the opposite direction, the dark path of evil, like a second life. And once he had set forth on it, no hope or ambition could be too great, because he really could do evil on a vast, inordinate, epoch-making scale, like a superhuman monster.

It was a consequence of age, not of some psychological tendency or inclination. Age and the experience that had built up over the years of his life. He had toyed momentarily with the other alternative: love. But he soon came to the conclusion that it was impossible. Love, in any of its forms, required the involvement of another person, and it was becoming clear to him that he had left all the others behind. This was something that he had to do on his own.

He ascended to untrodden heights, to the summit of the cosmos, abode of the great forces that move all things, beyond the realm of life. Who said he was just a corrupt policeman? And what if he was? Even confined to the meanest of forms, even if he was nothing more than a stray bundle of policeman's atoms, he could still channel the supreme powers of evil and create a new universe, a new city for himself, the hidden city, of which he would be king and god.

The heavens were bursting, their lights spinning crazily, the divine gas igniting in icy flames as the black throats let out their roars, which were echoed by a groan of exaltation exploding from the lips of Ignacio Cabezas.

IX

MAXI WENT ON LEADING THIS DISJOINTED PARADE FOR a long time; there seemed to be no end to his meandering, and yet, at the same time, it was speeding up. Finally the chapter of rummaging came to a close, and the scavengers whom Maxi was helping turned homeward. Once they crossed Directorio, the whole family climbed up onto the cart, and their human draught horse started trotting through the dim labyrinth of the projects, following the little streets that led toward the shantytown. As he passed under the streetlamps at the corners, the stalkers glimpsed his sweaty form. His mouth was open—he must have been panting—and he was so intent on his task that he didn't look back once. Which was just as well because with the frequent flashes of lightning the girls—who were half a block behind with nowhere to hide—were clearly visible in silhouette. They in turn were so worried about being noticed by Maxi that they never thought to look around, so they didn't see the car that was coming up behind them in first gear, stopping at every corner. The street was otherwise empty, and when the lightning relented the darkness thickened. A massive wind had risen, blowing in all directions, chaotically. The plants in the little gardens were thrashing about madly, throwing off leaves and buds like a frenzied gambler tossing dice.

Suddenly, in a paroxysm of thunder and lightning, the rain came crashing down. Thousand of gallons of water fell at once, in black swells heaved about by the wind, which collided with resounding wallops. Jessica and Vanessa were horrified to see the cart ahead of them accelerating suddenly. It was getting away, leaving them there, exposed to the elements, with nowhere to shelter ... or so they thought. Headlights suddenly lit them up, and they heard a roaring, distinct from the noise of the storm, approaching till it almost touched them: it was the furious acceleration of a car, and then the squeal of brakes. Jessica jumped aside so as not to be struck by the door swinging open.

"Get in!" shouted an urgent voice from inside.

The two girls screamed like banshees, and their shrill notes spiraled up among the torrents inextricably, although they were screaming for different reasons: Jessica because the storm, although it hadn't come as a surprise, had made her quite hysterical; Vanessa because, in the greenish light from the dashboard dials, she had recognized the bestial face craning forward to look up at them. It was the hideous man who had stopped her in the street, the stalker from her worst nightmares. It was so unexpected, and at the same time so horrifyingly opportune, that her whole being was seized by a spasm of terror, and she saw him as a bloodthirsty stegosaurus hoisting his rocky neck from a lake of oil, on the night of the end of the world. The escalation of her cries was answered by more crackling flashes in the sky and Jessica's continued shrieking, which made Vanessa scream more loudly still because she thought her friend had recognized him too. And their notes at the very top of the scale were accompanied by the policeman's hoarse bass, shouting angrily:

"Get in, you stupid bitches! Get in, for fuck's sake, or I'll blow you away!" As if he really would, he began to fumble at his chest, near his armpit, but the nervous tension in the air had flustered him as well, and he fell forward onto the passenger seat. When he lifted his face again, a moment later, it was even more horrible and distorted than before. And when he pulled his hand from underneath his body, and reached out toward the girls, almost touching them, it wasn't a gun he was holding but a small crystal flask, streaming with rain, from which the lightning struck scarlet sparks.

"GET IN!!"

Whether spellbound by the ruby flask, which seemed to make the rain more liquid in the space around it, or frightened by that madman's anger, or because they really had nowhere else to go and were getting soaked, the girls obeyed. They had been warned so often, ever since they could remember, against the temptation of getting into a stranger's car, there was really no excuse for yielding to it now. But people quite often do exactly what they shouldn't, automatically ignoring every sensible and reasonable course of action. And the man wasn't actually a stranger, which is what made it really strange. Unfortunately Vanessa was stuck in the middle, between her friend and the policeman, and this would lead to mutual recriminations later on: Vanessa would say that she had been pushed in by Jessica, who would claim, in all sincerity, that she had simply followed Vanessa's lead. In any case, once they were in, Cabezas stretched out his arm in front of them and yanked the door shut as he stepped on the accelerator and released the clutch. The car shot away.

"Do you remember me?"

Vanessa had lost her voice somewhere in the back of her throat but finally she found it again:

"Yeah. You're Cynthia's dad, right?"

The familiarity of her tone wasn't really surprising; she had the manners of a typical convent-school girl.

In the darkness, Jessica's face twisted into a grimace of astonishment. She had met Ignacio Cabezas, Cynthia's father, and this wasn't him. Vanessa must have been getting mixed up. But when she heard him say, "That's right," the first thing she thought was that he must have been the father of a different Cynthia, and since there was a girl at their school with that name, apart from the one who got killed, Jessica guessed that she was this man's daughter. In any case, it was a relief to learn that there was some connection, and she relaxed a bit, but not for long.

"Where were you going, in a storm like this?"

"We were going home," said Vanessa.

"Don't lie! You think I was born yesterday?"

"I swear!"

"Save your swearing, little Miss Innocent! You were following your brother."

Jessica intervened, not because she wanted to help her friend but because she hated to be left out of a conversation:

"We wanted to find out what he was doing, how far he goes with the collectors."

"And you had to do it tonight? In the rain?"

"How were we supposed to know it was going to pour?"

It was a good answer; a moment of silence ensued. The car was plowing through a choppy sea (the streets had flooded), throwing up big curved screens of water on either side. Cabezas drove boldly, taking the corners at top speed, as if he were on a race track.

"Where are we going?"

"Don't you worry; we'll be waiting for him when he gets there. I know where he's going, even if you don't."

"You know Maxi?"

"You two are going to introduce me. I'd like to say a few words to him."

That explained it all satisfactorily, so now it was just a matter of waiting for events to unfold. The windshield wipers were shucking masses of water off the glass, without really improving the visibility. Vague and shifting shapes could be glimpsed through the momentarily transparent semicircles, and the beams of the headlights vanished into the raging whirl. That's why the girls stared with saucer-like eyes when the car, which was still accelerating, came out into an open space of some kind, and they saw a dawn-like radiance ahead, rising up to the clouds. They were dazzled and shaded their eyes with their hands. It was a ring of yellow light, or rather a dome, made of pure illuminated night air, in which millions of moving points created a golden texture with a marvelous depth.

"What's that?" they shouted.

"The shantytown," said Cabezas.

"Are they bees?" asked Vanessa.

"No, you moron!" said Jessica. "They're raindrops."

When their gazes descended from this wonder, they discovered that they were in a very wide, completely flooded avenue (it would never have occurred to them that it was Calle Bonorino, the street on which they lived). It was a rectangular lake, its surface ruffled by gusts of wind and pricked by rain. There was, of course, no longer any difference between street and sidewalk; both were under water. But it looked as though there was no sidewalk on the right anyway, because there were no houses on that side, just a broad parking lot for trucks and a very long wall. And in the middle of that desolate, rainswept space was a motionless figure, which they all noticed at the same time. Although their vision of this person through the windshield sluiced with water was dim and blurry, all three were sure they knew who it was.

"There he is!" shouted Cabezas, wrenching the steering wheel around with all his strength. "What did I tell you? How'd he get here so quick, the bastard!"

But as they drove toward him, he looked wrong in the headlights, and even Cabezas had to admit that Maxi couldn't have beaten them on foot. Vanessa was the first to see who it really was:

"It's the Pastor!"

At the same time, succumbing to a resurgence of hysteria, Jessica yelled:

"Careful! Don't run him over!"

The two cries entered the inspector's consciousness simultaneously, and their effect was to set him thinking. He also took his foot off the accelerator and stepped on the brake, and since the vehicle wasn't responding as well as it would have on dry ground, gave the steering wheel a spin. The car pulled up right next to the Pastor, who was drenched to the bone and clearly resigned to it. He was young, chubby, dark-skinned, and had the look of an Indian from the Andean plateau. He was trying to see who was in the car, but couldn't because of the tinted windows and the dazzling headlights, so in his uncertainty he maintained a politely expectant attitude. He had apparently been waiting for someone, but must have begun to suspect that the person he had arranged to meet was not in the car.

"So this is the famous Pastor," said Cabezas. "The one who sells drugs to you lot. No wonder you were scared I'd run him over."

"No!" shouted Jessica. "I just didn't want him to get hurt. I've never seen him before."

"And you?"

"I've seen him around, that's all. He's always going to the police station near my place . . . I've never bought anything from him!"

Cabezas's mind was racing, as if it had taken over from the motor of his car, which had now come to a stop. For him this chance encounter was like winning the lottery. But he was also realizing how much he didn't know. So his colleagues in the police force were in contact with the Pastor? What a time to find out! They were using the Pastor as an informer, behind his back, but it was really a way of getting into the trade, which was supposed to be his area; tacitly, they'd let him have free rein, just so he could flail around without cracking the secret, and then, when the time was ripe, they would use him as a scapegoat. They were going behind his back . . . and the judge's back too, because they'd put her on his trail, knowing it wouldn't lead anywhere.

But now by the most amazing and fantastic stroke of luck he had come to the place that no one had thought he could reach on his own, where no one wanted him to be: the very center of the action. There must have been a reason why that scarecrow was standing out there in the rain. Maybe the storm was the signal the Bolivians had been waiting for to launch their big operation. Or maybe not. Maybe the signal was something else entirely. But that didn't matter: by the power of sheer action he could shape the circumstances to fit any format. All he had to do was collect the prize for his triumphant decision to be bad, or to occupy what was left of his life—as a liquid fills a receptacle—with the hyperplastic element of evil.

He opened the door and got out. His mind was made up. Getting wet was the least of his worries.

"Praise be to the Lord!" he shouted at the top of his lungs, so he could be heard over the thunder and the crashing of the rain.

"Praise be, brother."

"Where is he?"

The Pastor stared at Cabezas open-mouthed, and since he was shorter and had to look up, his face was doused with water.

"Come on, where is he? They're right behind us!"

"But who sent you?"

Of all the plausible replies, Cabezas chose the one that he could back up with something concrete and visible. And, by chance, he hit on just the thing to fool the Pastor:

"They brought me," he said, pointing at the car. The Pastor bent down a little, and a flash of lightning revealed two pale faces looking at him. He recognized Vanessa.

"He's in duckling, number seventeen," he said with obvious relief. "But he's fine ..."

Then Cabezas made his big mistake. It was understandable: Comissioner Cuá, the chief at Police Station Seventeen, had a surname that sounded like a duck's quack. Thinking that the Pastor was referring to his colleague, Cabezas asked ingenuously:

"So how do we get the gear out of the station?"

Grasping the enormity of the misunderstanding, the Pastor took a step back and his expression morphed.

"You're not the father! You're a cop!"

Then it was his turn to make a fatal mistake. He put his hand in his pocket. He wasn't reaching for anything. It was just a habit. Something he'd picked up from preaching: he'd learnt that the more absurd and unnecessary a gesture, the greater its effect on the audience. Cabezas, who thought the Pastor was reaching for a gun, whipped his out first and fired two shots into the young man's chest. The Pastor toppled over backward, like a tree-trunk falling into the enormous puddle. Almost as soon as his victim's head hit the water, Cabezas was back at the wheel of his car, accelerating wildly, ignoring the shrieks of his passengers and the hair-raising hissing of the lightning bolts, and the hammering of the rain on the hood, and the sirens of the police cars arriving at the scene of the crime. For the moment, all he wanted was to get out of there and if he'd been near the ultimate edge, the black rim of the universe, he would have aimed the snout of the car in that direction and driven off.

X

THE FLOATING CORPSE WAS NOT YET COLD WHEN AN IM-
pressive squad of new-model patrol cars came tearing out of the
narrow part of Bonorino in single file and pulled up on the esplanade, with their sirens blaring in a raucous *ostinato* and their
lights flashing relentlessly. The cars at the rear rushed forward in
a final spurt of acceleration while the front-runners were already
braking. They ended up forming a large semi-circle all pointing
at the body. For a moment nothing moved, except for the lights
spinning on the roofs of the cars. The rain went on lashing this
urban plateau. It seemed to be running off the great dome of light
over the shantytown to swell the black floodwaters converging
on the corpse.

The first thing to move was the door of the car that had ended
up in the middle. A moment later, the doors of all the other cars
opened too. But no one got out. The doors stayed open, swinging on their hinges in empty space. If the door of the middle
car had closed again, perhaps all the others would have followed
suit. But it didn't. A leg emerged. It was the leg of a woman: fat,
short, but shapely. A stocking with a pearly sheen, a red leather
shoe with a stiletto heel at least six inches high. Legs emerged

from all the other cars, one per door, but these were men's legs, in trousers of regulation blue, with feet encased in impeccably polished boots. All of the feet, like the first to emerge, hesitated for a moment in the air, thrust out almost horizontally, as if to say: "Shall I take the plunge?" In any case, they were drenched already; not just wet, but pummeled and wrung by the rain.

The little red shoe plunged into the water, followed by the matching shoe, and then, in a single fluid movement (it only took a couple of seconds, and yet it had a certain choreographic grandeur), there was a woman standing beside the car. It was the implacable and widely feared Judge Plaza. The rain renewed its attack on her. Policemen had stepped from each of the cars, all looking respectfully in the same direction as the judge.

She was an extraordinarily short woman and obese, aged somewhere between forty and fifty, with dyed-blond hair (it was naturally dark), and Indian or perhaps partly African features. Very confident, well-groomed, commanding and decisive. She had earned her reputation. She inspired fear. The tabloid journalists loved her, and so did their huge audience, who felt it was time for a tough and energetic justice, unhampered by wigs and precedents, ready to take to the streets and fight crime on its own turf.

A few die-hard liberals criticized Judge Plaza—under their breath, mind you, and among themselves in their ivory towers— for being a "media celebrity." But that wouldn't have stopped them approving of her if she hadn't been so vulgar, so in tune with the bloodthirsty instincts of the masses. In fact they had a very good reason to approve of her, which was that she always chose her prey among the masses that had made her a star. And once she had chosen and the hunt was on, she was as fierce as a wild cat: relentless, vengeful, truly bad, of that you could be sure. There was no escape. The public cheered and cried out for more. It's odd that it never occurred to those citizens, not even for a moment, as they sat in front of their televisions following the judge's exploits, that one day she might target them. After all, anyone can end up looking suspicious, given the complexity of modern life in a big city, and she was not the sort of judge to bother with gathering evidence, or comparing witness statements, or giving guarantees; her specialty was destruction, annihilation, and the slightest suspicion or rumor was enough for her to go on. She was a woman to be feared, yet none of her fans was afraid of her. Maybe it was because of her status as a media personality. The villains she was after were personalities too, at least as soon as she was on the case, and the whole operation remained within the kingdom of images. Why would the viewers feel that this spectacle had anything to do with their physical reality? They might as well have believed that someone from the TV was going to call them and give them a huge cash prize or a car or a trip to the Caribbean. Nobody really expects that to happen. It's often said that television has changed people's lives, but the truth is that life has maintained its independence.

The water was almost up to her knees, which were closer to the ground than those of ordinary mortals. She started walking forward. Her men gathered around her. The judicial police officers under her command were an elite group: experienced, incorruptible, bound together by a samurai mysticism and a blind obedience to the judge, who rewarded their loyalty by providing them with the latest, most sophisticated arms and granting them an autonomy that they exploited to the full. According to the legend, each of the judge's men had a thousand revolvers.

The corpse was floating at the vortex of the group's collective attention, the judge's having magnetized that of all her men. It was something more than attention. They had never seen her like this before, although they weren't actually looking at her. The floating point in the dark water reflected everything.

One of the judge's most famous and frequently misunderstood declarations was that her only aim in life was to bequeath to the world, at the end of her brief sojourn, something it had not possessed before. It sounded like a throwaway line, the kind of thing that people trot out when they're stuck for something to say, but it was more subtle than that. For a start, it's not so simple to bring something new into the world: it's a bit like bringing a rock back from the moon, except that these days the moon is really a part of the world. And she wasn't referring to a combination of pre-existing elements or a rearrangement, but to something really new, a new element, which could enter into old combinations, if anyone so desired. This was a strange ambition for a judge: justice is like a zero-sum game; you could say that its mission, the essence of what it does, is to transform a situation without affecting the overall number of elements. Adding something new is more like what art does.

On the other hand, no one could have been surprised by the judge's evocation of life's brevity. She wasn't old (around fifty and well preserved), but she was at the center of the action, right in the line of fire. Hundreds of criminals were out to get her, and whatever precautions are taken in such a case, they are never sufficient. At that fateful moment, on the flooded esplanade, a thought occurred simultaneously to each of her men: "They'll have to kill us all to get to her." And yet, at the same time, they knew that someone, inconceivably, had breached the protective wall.

The lightning was intensifying. The storm had not abated; on the contrary. Wild shudders ran back and forth over the surface of the water, and the floating corpse danced, as if on a short-circuiting electric bed, arching and writhing like a sleeper in the grip of a horrible nightmare.

"To leave something new and different in the world, after my brief residence, something to enrich the lives of those to come ..." Yes, but to do that, wouldn't she have to die? And wasn't death the destruction of everything, the new as well as the old? The judge's aspiration associated the old with the individual, while the new was seen as a legacy to the species as a whole, which meant that death, when it came, would be something positive.

But death, in this case, had arrived ahead of time, nobody really understood how.... And precisely because they didn't understand, they knew that a revelation was imminent. Just at that moment the television crews arrived, and the news girls, followed by cameramen, came rushing and splashing up to the judge, who had begun to walk toward the corpse, stiffly upright as if in a trance.

Thanks to some miracle of communication, the event had already been "deciphered" by the time the ad hoc retinue reached the dead man's feet, and big red phosphorescent letters appeared on the television screens, over the images from the live coverage: JUDGE PLAZA'S SON MURDERED or MURDER VICTIM JUDGE'S SON, or something like that. This was a real news story, sensational and surprising, especially since until that moment no one had even suspected that the judge had a son, or that she had been married. It had been assumed, in fact, that she had no family or friends, or any kind of private life: she slept on a sofa in her office at the courthouse, never took a day off or a vacation; it was inconceivable that she might be subject to commonplace emotions or enmeshed in conventional relationships. And now, suddenly ... an amazing turn of the screw had confirmed her superhuman capacity to generate news, this time with a revelation that went "straight to the heart": she was a mother, a mother facing the ultimate loss, the loss of her only child.

The news girls thrust their microphones at her mouth, shouting barely audible questions over the roar of the storm. The rain, falling more heavily than ever, bounced off the big black foam covers of the mikes, and splashed in the judge's face, which was white as chalk. The cameramen kept turning from the judge to the corpse and back, and the glaring spotlights attached to their cameras made shadows dance on the water.

Any creature equipped with a rudimentary cerebral cortex would have been able to deduce the inner workings of the crime. But the news girls didn't operate like that. It's not that they were stupid (not that stupid anyway), but in their work, for the truth to count as true it had to emerge laboriously from a background of error. There was a logic to it as well: they had to get everything wrong to keep people talking and thereby justify their role. That was why they asked:

"Did your son, the Pastor, have a real religious vocation, or was he using it as a cover for dealing drugs?"

"How could he have sunk so low? Where did you go wrong, Judge Plaza?"

"Were you aware of your son's illegal activities?"

"Who do you suspect, Judge Plaza?"

The questions were calculated to provoke a declaration. Such was the violence of the rain that as soon as the judge opened her mouth, it filled with water. But she spat it out vigorously and shouted:

"He wasn't a drug dealer! He wasn't a Pastor! He wasn't anything like that! He was my son! He was helping me with the investigation, in spite of the risks. He was brave and audacious and he was prepared to lay down his life to protect the community. He was the first to fall because he was in the front line."

"Did he have time to tell you what he had found out, Judge Plaza?"

"Everything! Everything! Now I'm the target. But it won't be so easy to kill me! From here on out, we're calling the shots, and he is the one who will have to die."

"Who, Judge Plaza? Do you know who was responsible?"

The judge hesitated almost imperceptibly, but quickly recovered her composure, and her voice became more guttural:

"It was a man well known to the police, a corrupt officer: Deputy Inspector Cabezas, from Station 38. It all goes through him, and we've had him under surveillance for some time. Up until now, I've treated him with respect because he's a father too. When his daughter died, I knew that the loss would eat away at him and sooner or later he'd slip up. Now he has made a fatal mistake, and we'll get him before the night is out, before it stops raining. He's cornered."

"Is he dangerous? Is he extremely dangerous? Will he kill again?"

"The man's a wild animal, he's desperate, and he's kidnapped two innocent teenagers!"

Then the judge broke down and bowed her head, seized by an uncontrollable fit of weeping. The cameramen stepped back to get her body into the frame, and the shadows rearranged themselves. The news girls withdrew their microphones because everything had been said, and they knew that the headlines would be coming up on the screens: CORRUPT POLICEMAN FATHER OF MURDERED GIRL. COUNTDOWN TO REVENGE. ALL WILL DIE.

The pause provided an opportunity for the obligatory cut to the other breaking story: the rain. The record for precipitation was about to be broken, and all the mobile news teams that the TV channels had sent out around the city were equipped with portable gauges made of transparent plastic, marked off in inches. The hourly rainfall had exceeded sixteen inches already, and was climbing to unprecedented levels. All the stations had diagrams in the corner of the screen showing the water level in the gauges rising in real time. In a city as large as Buenos Aires, rainfall is often heavier in certain areas than in others, and at that moment, by a curious coincidence, the heaviest falls were occur-

ring on the esplanade at the end of Calle Bonorino. The news
girls made the most of this, especially since the record for the
volume of water that had fallen on the capital would be broken
in a few minutes' time. Nature happened to be making history at
precisely the point in space and time where this particular story
was unfolding.

And there was blood in the water. The blood of a son. A single
drop. As in the most potent homeopathic remedies, one drop
was enough to alter the chemical and philosophical composition
of that nocturnal Styx. The water took on a shadowy pink over-
tone, visible only to the mind's eye in the prevailing blackness.

Certain incidental shots elicited other reflections, albeit in
an unconscious or subliminal way, particularly the ones that
showed the judge standing in the rain without an umbrella or
any kind of protection. Except in the movies, no one stands out
in a downpour like that, as if they hadn't noticed; it's a basic
human reflex to seek shelter. Therefore she wasn't human. The
story was taking a new turn.

The TV channels were in a frenzy. They had found photos of
Cabezas in their digital archives and they were alternating them
with the live images. For some reason his face was horribly distorted by the electronic medium, becoming more grotesque
with every passing second. It must have been because they were
still scrambling to find real photographs and making do with art-
ist's impressions. But new images kept coming from the archives:
an identity photo of Cynthia Cabezas; shots from her funeral,
with the girls from Misericordia, and her parents in tears. And
then, all of a sudden: old photos of Cabezas and Judge Plaza at

some night spot, looking young, holding glasses of champagne;
the Pastor preaching to a congregation; the judge with her son in
her arms, when he was just a few months old; Cynthia as a little
girl on the beach with her parents.... And the night, the rain,
the city seen from helicopters—all the channels had sent one
out—an ocean of confusion, from which the ghostly face of Cabezas reemerged, grimacing, it seemed.... A birthday party ten
years ago, with Cynthia and the child who would grow up to be
the Pastor at the head of the table, wearing paper hats.... Once
again, the theme of life's brevity, this time in the world of images.
And it was taken to an extreme by the fantasy that was hovering
over the viewers at that moment: an intergalactic traveler arrives
in a strange world without any kind of protection (what protection could he have?). The environmental conditions are totally
hostile to life: he's doomed, obviously; he's going to die in a few
tenths of a second; you could say he's as good as dead.... And
yet, for the time being, he's alive, arriving in the world, in the
world's horrific reality. And "the time being" is all there is.

XI

MEANWHILE, CABEZAS HADN'T GONE VERY FAR WITH his two passengers. In the end, the edge of the world was too remote; it couldn't be reached within this life, and after the first moment of panic, he hadn't really intended to try. He went around behind the cemetery and the Piñeyro Hospital and headed east on Avenida del Trabajo. The land sloped steeply down toward what is appropriately called "Lower" Flores, and as the water rose to the tops of the wheels, Cabezas realized that if he couldn't drive at top speed, he didn't really feel like driving at all, so he might as well stop. He thought that perhaps he should make a decision before getting too far away. Or maybe it wasn't as rational as that: something was holding him back, keeping him within the circle where things were happening. There was still a lot to be sorted out, and the further away he was, the harder it would be. So he pulled up at the corner of Carabobo and pointed to the little pizzeria:

"We're going to have a coffee and calm down," he said, as if they'd gone out for a spin. The girls were too rigid with fear to react, so he invented a detail to make it more convincing: "You can walk back home from here when it stops raining."

This sounded plausible, even though the end of the rain seemed a world away. They got out and made a dash for it. The place was empty, except for a pair of sweethearts holding hands and talking in whispers, their gazes oscillating between the windows and the television over the door. The newcomers sat down at a table and stared at the screen. The show was just beginning.

They saw it all. Cabezas was so fascinated by what was happening on the television and by his own thoughts that the girls could have slipped away without him noticing, but oddly enough it seemed that they were in no hurry to be gone. It was still raining just as heavily, and they didn't want to get wet; given the state they were in, a trivial consideration like that mattered more than being at the mercy of a man described by the reporters as a dangerous criminal. Also, they didn't want to miss any of the dramatic events unfolding on the screen.

Although Cabezas had been waiting for the judge to pronounce his name, when she did, he couldn't help whispering, "The bitch!" But what came next was more surprising. It was obvious that they really were getting him mixed up with the father of Cynthia Cabezas; they'd spun a whole plot out of that misinformation. For some time he'd been haunted, as the hunted often are, by the old idea that he was caught up in a case of "mistaken identity." When he heard the judge's words and saw the old pictures on the television, the idea took on monstrous proportions: not just huge, but deformed. It wasn't that they had mixed him up with another man, leaving his true identity aside; they knew who he was and they were still mistaking him for someone else. If he'd been a better sport, he might have admitted that he had it coming because he was the one who'd started the confusion. But he wasn't in the mood for subtleties like that.

He looked on helplessly as the images followed one another, and the error reinforced itself and spread. He began to wonder how far it could go. Could it go all the way round and come back to bite the tail of the truth from which it had departed? The only way to stop it expanding would have been to impose a universal silence.... And the human race wasn't going to stop talking. There was no point trying to set the record straight. Once a misunderstanding was out there, it couldn't be reeled back in. The only solution was to make the best of it and press on, improvising all the way. Somehow, things worked out in the end, mysteriously enough. Even so, a feeling of deep despondency had come over him, due in part to the fierce insistence of the rain, both on the television and outside the windows of the pizzeria. The water was still rising. That sea of error: the world. And he had to keep going, on and on, burdened with all the solipsisms of his sloppy thinking and a mass of information drawn exclusively from television, bits and pieces as random as the sequence of episodes in a dream. He had to keep fleeing forward, but to where? What would become of him? Was he destined to be an eternal fugitive, eternally forbidden to look back? His despondency was deepening and coming to seem inflexibly ordained. This line of thought led him to the conclusion that his case was irremediable; after all, only the human could be remedied ...

Meanwhile on the esplanade, where everyone had paused to respect a mother's pain, the action was resuming. The cameras focused on Judge Plaza again, and she regained her fighting spirit. The manhunt was beginning: the judge and all her officers disappeared into their cars, in one of which they stowed the corpse, and drove off leaving boiling wakes in the big choppy lake that had covered the avenue. The breathless commentaries of the news girls, who were following the police in their various trucks, explained that they were heading for the nearby shantytown, which was still crowned with a great dome of light. According to the television—which is the very essence of action and therefore never wrong—the judge had ordered her samurais to take up positions all around the edge, and as soon as the perimeter was secured, she would go in herself, leading the way, armed to the teeth, ready to kill or die.

An unforgettable spectacle was about to unfold. The broadcast was charged with anticipation: millions of viewers were following the events in real time. The rain had broken all the records and its density and violence were still increasing. The shantytown must have been flooded, but the action was rushing on regardless, without waiting for conditions to return to normal. The apocalyptic downpour was becoming a mere backdrop to the adventure: people were beginning to act as if it were some kind of special effect.

And the rain served as a bridge to convey the sense of adventure because it was raining both on the scene where the events were taking place and on the houses of the people who were following the coverage; the rain was beating on the roofs and the walls, seeping in under the doors.... Cabezas shifted on his seat and noticed that there was water underfoot. The floor of the pizzeria was submerged. The streets outside were a sea: the water was already up to the windows of his car, which was parked in front of the door. Twice a minute, flashes of lightning lit up the scene.

Cut to the helicopters, which had reached the shantytown and were circling over it. The view was dizzying because of the height, the movement and the darkness. It had been a feat, as the commentators were quick to point out, to fly there in that weather, defying the rain, the headwinds and the lightning. The blades were spinning in a mass of almost solid water. The uncontrollable lurching resulted in shots of the nightbound city in which the horizon was vertical or sloping, sometimes even upside down. You could also see the other helicopters battling with the elements, and gauge what the storm was doing to them. SUICIDE MISSION TO BRING YOU THE NEWS, said the lettering on the screen, leaving nothing to the imagination.

Nevertheless, the airborne cameras kept aiming downward, and were able to provide vertical views of the shantytown from about seven hundred feet directly above its center. You could see the whole circle traced out in those famous, over-abundant lights, each little bulb a twinkling signal fixed in the rain-drenched darkness.

Quite apart from the unusual circumstances, the spectacle was interesting from an intellectual and aesthetic point of view. No one had ever seen the shantytown like that, in its entirety. It was a ring of light, with clearly marked lines going in at an angle of 45 degrees to the circumference, none of them leading to the center, which was dark, like a void. These "geometrical" shots were brief because of the buffeting, but also because they were interrupted by images from the ground, where, like amphibious creatures, the patrol cars were speeding along, followed by the news trucks, and taking up positions all around the shantytown. Nevertheless, the shots from overhead kept getting clearer. The ring was not evenly bright, but composed of ribbons and twirls: a profusion of tiny figures that, given more time and tranquility, the eye might have been able to decipher.

Suddenly, Cabezas let out a startled cry. He had been visited by a sudden "illumination" and not just metaphorically. A complete and convincing solution to the enigma that had resisted him for years was swimming into view. It was all thanks to the aerial shots, the "electrical map"—and, of course, the corresponding synapses in his brain. The broadcast that he was watching had also played its modest part: the style of the news channels, superposing images and text, favored or rather maximized redundancy. Once the picture was complete, it all seemed so clear, so utterly self-evident. When you tuned into that frequency, titles began to appear over your own mental images, and that was enough to throw a powerful light on the old mysteries. In this case, the caption that lit up in Cabezas's brain said: THE PATTERNS OF LIGHTS ARE USED TO IDENTIFY THE STREETS OF THE SHANTYTOWN. Those quirky garlands of bulbs—no two the same—at the entrance to each oblique street were "names" in a code that the dealers had been using, quite openly, to guide their clients. The system was foolproof: they used names that were easy to remember (like "the square," "the triangle," "the parallel lines," or "the hair"), changed the location every night, or several times a night, and waited until the buyers were already circling the shantytown before calling them on their cell phones to tell them where to go.

But it was like the Nazca lines: the inspector had been able to discover the pattern only by seeing the whole thing from the air, as no one had ever seen it before. Most of the dealers in the shantytown were from Peru or Bolivia, and they may have drawn inspiration from that Pre-Colombian land art, adding electricity to bring it up to date, or maybe they were using an ancestral communication technique whose secrets had been handed down from generation to generation.

Not only was the system as a whole revealed to him in its abstract form; thanks to the Pastor's fatal mistake, Cabezas also knew where the proxidine had been stashed that night. "Seventeen duckling" ... the "duckling" was obviously a configuration of lights at the entrance to a street, and "seventeen" referred to a particular shack. He had seen the roughly painted numbers and he even thought he remembered, somewhere on the perimeter, a string of lights that looked like a duck in profile. It wouldn't be hard to find, anyhow. And the Pastor had died before he could tell anyone that Cabezas knew the address. So the proxidine would still be there ...

By association, this insight led to memories of the magical drug whose benefits he had so liberally enjoyed. And that was when the last pieces of the puzzle fell into place. As well as kicking himself about the street signs—"Why didn't I see it before?"—now he was thinking, "How could I have forgotten the proxidine!" This was yet another confirmation of the method on which he had based his police career, which consisted of keeping all the relevant data in play at once. It was the only way to solve a case, and if on this occasion he had abandoned it momentarily, and as a consequence lost heart, he did at least have an excuse: the situation was truly exceptional; he was staking his fate on a single card. In fact, he hadn't altogether forgotten about the proxidine but he had only been considering its exchange value. Now, remembering its intrinsic value, he realized, finally, that it held the key. Because the drug's much-touted effect, which was to increase the proximity of things, applied above all to the elements of a problem: by bringing them into sudden contiguity, it brought them closer to the solution.

Of course! The proxidine! What was he thinking? And suddenly it was there, within reach.... Although it wouldn't be quite that easy. He still had to go and get it. He had a vague hunch that it wasn't just the regular stash they needed for a night of dealing. There was a reason why they had all decided to launch a final offensive, in spite of the rain: himself, the judge, those two brats, and the Pastor.... True, some were following others (he had followed the girls, for example), but it wasn't a vicious circle. The Pastor wouldn't have been standing there on the esplanade in the rain unless something special was happening. And to have reached the scene of the crime two minutes after her son's death, the judge must have set out well in advance, with all her men, too, armed for battle. The Pastor must have been waiting to tell her about the location of the shipment—and instead he had told Cabezas. Even the television crews must have been tipped off.... They had their own contacts, as well as being big consumers (a while back one of the networks had been accused of running a subliminal ad campaign for proxidine because of its slogan: "the news up close").

A big shipment ... or something better: the mother of all drugs. Cabezas had heard of "super-pure proxidine"; people were always talking about it, but he'd never really stopped to think about what it might mean. Perhaps it was unthinkable. The expression itself was hyper-redundant. But the thing to which those senseless words referred was his talisman, the only thing left that could free him from the judge's fatal embrace.

By going back to the shantytown, he would, of course, be putting his head in the lion's mouth. He did, however, have the advantage of knowing exactly where to go, and with the confusion produced by the manhunt as well as the rain, his chances of slipping in under the radar were, paradoxically, better than ever.

He had made up his mind. He got to his feet, then noticed the two girls sitting at the table. That pair of airheads still hadn't run away! Just as well: he could use them to create a diversion. He took his cell phone out of his pocket and put it on the table:

"Listen carefully. When the rain stops, go home. But first, right now, or as soon as I'm gone, call the judge and tell her that I'm not holding you hostage, you're free, and I've gone to Paraguay; tell her to catch me if she can." He paused for a moment, then added: "All you have to do to call the judge's secret number is hit zero."

He splashed out the door. The current outside was so strong it almost toppled him. But he reached his car, got in, started it, and drove away gunning the engine and parting the waters, like a new Moses.

XII

AS SOON AS THE KILLER POLICEMAN WAS GONE, VANESSA astonished her friend, who had already opened her mouth and was about to launch into a commentary on what had just happened, by demanding silence with a peremptory gesture and turning toward the table where the pair of sweethearts were sitting, still holding hands, as silent as two objects.

"Heddo," she said, and tried again, grimacing, but without any more success, on the contrary: "Geddgo ... leglo ..." Then, finally, she got it right: "Hello!" She apologized with a smile: the nervous tension had made her tongue go numb. "I didn't say hello before because I didn't want that madman to notice you. Do you know who it was? Did you hear him?"

"Ma'am, yes," said Adelita—it was her.

Jessica turned her head with a look of shock and horror, as if to say: "This is too much! If there's one more twist in the plot ..." And perhaps her dismay was justifiable. As a beekeeper may be killed by just one more sting because of all the toxins that have accumulated in his system, although a bee sting in itself is almost harmless, there may be a limit to the quandaries that a mind can accommodate. Vanessa, who was more than willing to explain now that she had recovered the ability to speak, enlightened her friend immediately:

"She works on the third floor in your building. She was the first person I turned to when this all started, don't you remember? I told you! The Pastor's friend ... which reminds me," she added, spinning around to face Adelita: "You know he's dead? He was killed by that guy who was here with us. We were witnesses."

"Ma'am, yes. I saw it on television," Adelita said, pointing at the screen. "But he wasn't my friend. You saw me walking with him, but that was the only time we ever spoke."

"And what did he say to you?"

"Ma'am, he told me to believe in Jesus and things like that. But I didn't listen."

"Good for you. It was all a front. Luckily the truth always comes out in the end."

Talking had restored Vanessa's confidence, and she wanted to regain control, to wrest the initiative away from the television. She went and sat down at the couple's table; Jessica followed. Perfunctory introductions were made:

"This is Jessica, my best friend. It was pure chance that we got dragged into this business."

"Hi."

"Hi," said Jessica.

"Hi," both girls said to the boy, who was fugly and insignificant and hadn't opened his mouth.

"This is Alfredo, my fiancé."

"Uhuh? You're engaged?" asked Vanessa in a slightly supercilious tone, thinking, "Birds of a feather."

"Ma'am, we were separated for a while but we got back to-gether again tonight, thanks to your brother."

"Maxi!? You know him?"

"Ma'am, yes. He's a saint."

"He's a saint," echoed the fiancé Alfredo, rustily, as if he had gone for years without speaking.

"Maxi, the things he does!" said Vanessa, shaking her head.

"He's really sweet," said Jessica. "But he's too naïve."

Adelita seemed to be on the point of stepping in to defend him, but she kept quiet. There was a silence. The four of them looked out of the windows: the storm had resumed in all its fury, as if it were starting over again, with a lavish festival of thun-der and lightning, and the rain pounding like millions of drums. They had to rest their feet on the crossbars of the chairs because the tiled floor was under four inches of water. The waiters were sitting on the bar. There was nothing to do but wait. Vanessa heaved a long sigh and said:

"Well, now that it's all over ..."

"Ma'am!" said Adelita, interrupting her. "If I may ... I don't think it's quite over yet."

"What do you mean?"

"I think your brother is in danger."

The look of shock on Vanessa's face expressed a bewilderment larger than the girl herself. It was as if she didn't even know who her brother was.

"Maxi?" It looked like she was going to say, "You know him?" again. But instead she said: "What's he got to do with it?"

"Maxi!" cried Jessica simultaneously. "Of course! We forgot about him! Where could he have got to?"

"What's it matter?" said Vanessa and added, addressing Adelita: "Don't worry about him. He might seem really vague but he knows how to look after himself. And even if he does get a bit wet, it won't do him any harm."

Adelita shook her head stubbornly.

"Ma'am, I wasn't talking about the rain. They found him a place to sleep in the shantytown because he couldn't stay awake."

Vanessa burst out laughing.

"He's such a baby. He falls asleep on his feet as soon as it gets dark." But thinking about it, she frowned. "Did they put him to bed?" And in an aside to Jessica: "I hope the sheets are clean. He's so fussy..."

"So what's the problem?" Jessica asked Adelita.

"Ma'am, I'm worried that the man who killed the Pastor might have gone to kill Maxi." The two girls gaped in amazement. "Because he was following him today, wasn't he?"

"We were following him. We wanted to see what he was doing. But Cabezas..." They looked at each other. "Come to think of it, it's suspicious the way he turned up right then. Could he have been following us?" They both spoke at once. "But why would he want to kill Maxi? And how would he find him, if he's asleep in a house in the shantytown?"

"Ma'am, it was the Pastor who hid Maxi and maybe he told that man something before he died. You didn't hear anything?"

"Yes," shouted Vanessa in a panic. "He gave him an address. Something with 'seventeen,' could that be right?"

"Ma'am, that's where he is," said Adelita in a dramatic tone of voice.

"Maxi's doomed, Vanessa! That madman's going to kill him! And it's our fault!"

"But he said he was going to Paraguay! And he won't go to the shantytown; that's where the Judge is looking for him ..."

"Ma'am, I think he was lying. Didn't you see that he headed off in the direction of the shantytown ..."

"That's true ..."

Alfredo jumped up, plunging his feet into the water.

"We have to go and warn Maxi! Come on, Adela!"

"No, wait a minute. We wouldn't get there in time."

"And we'd drown on the way," said Jessica.

In spite of everything, Alfredo was ready to rush off, but Adelita grasped his arm.

"I've got an idea." She pointed to the cell phone that Cabezas had left on the other table. The two girls looked at it too.

"We forgot to call the judge!" exclaimed Vanessa. "We can call her now and tell her to protect Maxi ..."

"Ma'am, she won't be able to do anything, but I can call the people who are hiding him ..."

They handed her the phone at once. She examined it for a moment, then punched in a number and lifted it to her ear.

Alfredo turned to the two middle-class girls and said confidentially:

"Adela's very intelligent. She always works things out. Since she came here from Peru, she's succeeded in everything. The only thing she couldn't do was find me. Luckily Mr. Maxi came along."

"Did you run away? How come? Were you scared of getting married?"

"Something like that. But it's all behind me now: water under the bridge."

"Well said."

Meanwhile, Adelita had been speaking in a shrill voice, very different from her usual whispering. She hung up and said:

"It's all sorted. They'll take care of it. I asked them not to wake him up. He's so tired, the poor thing . . ."

Jessica and Vanessa smiled, imagining the scrawny little guys from the shantytown carrying Maxi's gigantic sleeping body. There'd have to be twenty of them at least.

"But will they be able do it in time? It's been a while since that criminal left, you know."

"Ma'am, they have all the time in the world." She seemed very calm about it all, and to put them at ease she said, "Didn't you notice how, earlier on, extra time was needed too, for Maxi to get to the shantytown when it started raining, and reunite me and Alfredo, and let the guys put him to bed, and then for the Pastor to get back to the esplanade?"

"That's true. We got there by car in a few seconds."

They relaxed. Now there really was nothing more to do. They looked idly at the television, which was showing a series of dim shots of the shantytown's outer alleys. Alfredo sighed:

"It's such a long time since I saw the old shantytown . . ." Adelita took his hand and squeezed it. The others were imagining that as soon as the rain stopped, the young couple would go there and consummate their delayed marriage. But was it ever going to stop raining?

"I just thought of something," said Jessica. "Shouldn't we call home?"

"You're right! My mom'll be having kittens. Is there a public phone here?"

She was already turning around to ask the waiters when she remembered that there was a cell on the table. Both girls laughed at her distraction; Vanessa picked it up and called. Her mother answered. Vanessa said that she and Jessica had been caught by the rain and taken shelter in a pizzeria where they were waiting for it to stop. They were fine; there was no reason to be worried. Yes, they'd got a bit wet, but it was no big deal. She didn't lie much, in the end, and given the circumstances a little white lying was justified. Her mother said something, and she pretended to remember Maxi (it wasn't just a pretense), and said that her brother, whom she'd run into by chance just as it was starting to rain, had gone to a friend's house and would probably spend the night there. She hung up with a sigh and passed the phone to Jessica, who called her mother and told her more or less the same story.

"Mothers..." they said to the other two, with a resigned smile. "You know what they're like."

"You're lucky to have them."

"But you have each other," said Jessica, "and you don't have to talk on the phone because you're together."

"Everyone has a mother, whether they like it or not," said Vanessa. "It's a mother's world. That's the only conclusion we can come to, in the end."

She looked at Jessica. Jessica looked at her, with a melancholy air. They were still living in a mother's world. Speaking of "conclusions," it was obvious that for Adelita and Alfredo, the adventure had come to an end, and it had ended well. They loved each other; they would get married and have children: they were home safe. But Vanessa and Jessica were still up in the air, faced with the never-ending choice between following the advice of their mothers and doing exactly the opposite. The only conclusion to be drawn from this or any other adventure was to let it be a lesson ... or not. That was the sole and dubious privilege of the middle class: not to learn from experience, to go on making mistakes, covered unconditionally by maternal insurance.

XIII

MAXI WAS SLEEPING IN A BIG FOLDING BED THAT THE shanty dwellers had constructed months before and stored in readiness for the time when it would come in useful. They had made it for him when they noticed how, as soon as night fell, he was overcome by sleepiness, rightly supposing that sooner or later he would end up staying a bit too late and be unable to go home. They might not have spoken to him but they had observed and studied him carefully, and so they were able to build a bed to measure. It was a sort of camp bed, made of coarse elastic fabric stretched over an aluminum frame, with four sets of hydraulic hinges. It had solid metal detachable feet, two feet high, arranged in three rows, one at either end and one in the middle. The shanty dwellers made a folding bed because it would have taken up too much space otherwise, and naturally they didn't want anyone but Maxi to use it. Plus it was easier to hide. They had also set aside a pair of linen sheets, and a vicuña-wool blanket, dyed bright red. These were never used either, in spite of which they were periodically taken to the laundry and the dry-cleaner's to keep them immaculate. They also carried out simulations every so often, to be sure that when the moment came they could unfold the bed and make it up in a few seconds. And there was always a shack empty somewhere to house it; they had a roster for every day of the year.

That night, when the Pastor came back from the esplanade with Maxi, who was wet and exhausted after having reunited the fiancés, the operation commenced immediately. They led him to the designated shack, and by the time he got there, stumbling along, seeing nothing, thunder crashing overhead, the bed was ready. He was fast asleep before his head touched the pillow.

The shack was an almost regular cube and the folding bed just fitted into it, pressing on the front and back walls. It was one of a million similar cubes, juxtaposed with or without gaps, sometimes crammed together in rows or bunches, haphazardly arranged in a vast collective improvisation. The amateur builders preferred simple forms, not for their aesthetic appeal or utility but precisely to simplify things. Simplification had a special meaning in the shantytown, as distinct from the rest of the city. In waking life, simple forms are very intellectual or abstract, but in the world of dreams they are simply practical or convenient. And this enormous ring belonged by right to the unconscious. The electricity cables, as numerous and chaotic as the buildings they connected, reinforced the shantytown's allegiance to the world of dreams.

Cabezas was driving around the ring road: the metaphor of the moth and the flame could not have been more apt. With the windshield wipers overwhelmed and the headlights under water, he could barely see where he was going. But the huge illuminated diamond of the shantytown was on his left, so he couldn't get lost. He had been around that circuit so many times, with the uneasy feeling that the mystery was just eluding his grasp, but all he had done was to make himself mysterious, without realizing! Now that he knew what he was looking for, he scrutinized each inward-leading street, checking the configurations of light bulbs suspended between the shacks. The bright patterns made him squint, even though he was seeing them through massive curtains of water. Everything was light in there, to the point where the light was reflecting itself.

Although his attention was narrowly focused, he couldn't help noticing that the "designs" formed by the light globes were "inside" others, which always had more or less the same shape, something like a lung. The attribution of a particular shape to a group of lights was disputable: they had to be joined up by an imaginary line, and with half a dozen lights or more, the joining could be done in many different ways.... If the idea was to indicate a location, it was paradoxical or counterproductive, but by the very nature of the medium, it couldn't be as simple as a sign saying HERE IT IS. Also, he had to remember that this was a part of the overall proxidine system.

He realized that the almost exaggerated brightness of the shantytown was due in part to the contrast with the surrounding darkness. Naturally, the electricity in the general area had been cut off because of the storm. But the shantytown wasn't affected because its power was diverted from the high tension cables that supplied the whole city, which never went down. And that was handy for the dealers, since their only method for guiding the buyers depended on electricity.

Finally Cabezas found the "duckling," as clear and obvious as a sunny day. He pulled up immediately. When he opened the door, the water was up to his waist; he almost had to swim. No sooner was he out than ten thousand bucketfuls of water came crashing down on his head. But it didn't bother him in the least. He had already adopted an amphibian attitude, and it all seemed perfectly natural. Everyone else was apparently reacting in the same way; it's amazing how quickly people adapt to extraordinary circumstances.

As soon as he entered the street, the news girls assailed him; they were everywhere. Wrapped in voluminous plastic capes, like the cameramen who were following them, and equipped with bulging goggles, they were indefinable monsters. The microphones they were holding out were also protected by waterproof hoods, and this abundance of plastic reflected the spotlights, turning the whole scene into a mobile accumulation of structures that seemed to be made of soft, crunchy glass. Guessing that they had mistaken him for one of the judge's men, Cabezas tried to throw them off the scent. Over their inept questions, he shouted:

"We've got him cornered on the other side of the shantytown, directly opposite here. I came to cut him off in case he slips through the net."

They rushed away, leaving him very satisfied with his trick. Indeed he felt that it vindicated his decision to be bad because now he had television on his side. But there was a risk that he hadn't considered: someone recognized him from the photos in the live coverage, and the police fell on him like hungry dogs. There were shots, and everyone started running. The images on the television screens went haywire, as they always do in this kind of situation. The cameramen took cover wherever they could, and aimed their cameras at an empty scene, interminably. This unchanging fixity was exacerbated by the fact that because of the suspense, and the fear of missing something important, the channels held off the ad breaks and kept the screen free of superimposed titles or images, leaving only the pure scenography of danger, in which, by definition, nothing could happen. For some reason, it was generally accepted that the lives of the cameramen were too precious for them to run the slightest risk. The only distraction was provided by the panting voices and nervous whispering of the news girls, hidden elsewhere, watching different scenes.

In this case there was, however, some movement: the movement of the water. It was flowing as well as falling. The streets of the shantytown had become foaming torrents, rushing away from the center toward the edges in a continuous cascade. This might have led one to suppose that the center was higher, but it was not. And in fact, it is not correct to say that the origin of those turbulent currents was "the center," since the streets did not converge toward the center of a circle, but ran obliquely, intersecting with the circumference at an angle of 45 degrees.

A couple of gunshots had cleared the way. Like an obese alligator swimming against the current, Cabezas went from shack to shack, gripping his pistol in both hands, staring at the roughly painted numbers on the doors. He didn't have to go very far. Just beyond the main garland of bulbs, in the shape of a duck, was number seventeen, in clear view. It was a cube like the rest, patched together from wood and tin, without windows or guttering. Inside lay the key to the impunity he longed for, or perhaps simply to happiness.

Meanwhile, Maxi was sleeping more deeply than ever. If it's true, as people say, that nothing is more soporific than the sound of rain beating on a roof, conditions were ideal, though he didn't really need any help. And the natural process had not been interrupted. No one had come to bother him; no one had entered his cubicle. But he must have been dreaming as never before. Unfamiliar beds make for more abundant dreaming because there are more physical disturbances for the dreamwork to interpret.

Cabezas hurled himself at the door, and the impact burst it wide open. He couldn't believe his eyes. Inside there was ... simply nothing. There was no room. It was a door in a facade, behind which stretched a desolate scene full of rain, with other shacks, near and far, illuminated by the lightning. It was similar and different at the same time: outside, but also inside. His first thought was that he should have expected it: nothing's ever that simple. But what could have gone wrong this time? The only explanation that occurred to him was that the Pastor had lied; but he hadn't, Cabezas was quite sure of that. "The dead don't lie," he said to himself. And yet the truth was also an abyss. He didn't have time to explore it because the judge appeared suddenly from the mouth of a dark alleyway, followed by her samurais. He raised his pistol thinking, "Goodbye proxidine," but before he could pull the trigger, she emptied the magazine of her submachine gun into his body, riddling it with at least a hundred bullets the size of dates. As he fell down dead, his eyes closed on the vision of that mysterious patio-like space.

What had happened? The Pastor had not lied, and no one had shifted Maxi. So? The boy's protectors had adopted a solution that was rather more complicated, but possible and logical in the circumstances. They changed the configurations of the lights in all the streets. Since they didn't know if Cabezas had memorized the series, they had to change them all so that he wouldn't get suspicious. They preserved the order, shifting everything six places, so the "duck" ended up shining over the entrance of the sixth street to the right, which is where the killer policeman went in hoping to find his treasure and found his ruin.

But did that mean that the shantytown could "spin"? Could that be possible? Perhaps it had been doing just that from time immemorial. Perhaps it had only ever existed as an endless rotation. Perhaps it was the famous "Wheel of Fortune," not standing up, as everyone imagined, but humbly laid on the ground, which would mean that it was no longer a matter of some riding high while others were cast down: everyone was low, all the time, simply changing places at ground level. There was no escaping poverty, and life was made up of little shifts which were insignificant in the end. Anyway, those tiny fractions of a revolution were extremely rare; they occurred once in a blue moon, by a combination of circumstances so complex that no one could unravel it. That was what had just happened, and no one had noticed. It was the only thing that the television couldn't cover, but the news teams had plenty to keep them busy.

News girls and cameramen had gathered around the body (the second one that night) and were waiting for a statement from the judge, who was quietly giving orders to her men. Finally she faced the cameras, and they thrust the microphones at her. Someone had opened an umbrella and was holding it over her head. Her words were broadcast live to the whole country:

"What we have seen here tonight is the demise of one of the most dangerous criminals to have threatened our national security in recent years. Let it be a warning to us, for the death of Inspector Cabezas does not mean the end of the proxidine problem; far from it—the problem has barely begun. He was a man of superior intelligence, perhaps the finest mind in Argentina: had he been able to use his gifts for good, he would have achieved great things, but he chose the infernal path of artificial contiguity. Many have been lured as he was, and sadly we can be sure that many more will follow. It is an endless slippery slope: people begin out of curiosity and end up killing in order to get to the "mother of all drugs." Everyone is drawn to her, rich and poor, men and women, old and young alike. The mass media have a categorical duty to make it clear to society as a whole that the "mother" cannot be reached. All efforts in that direction are futile, at least within a human lifespan. You and your colleagues have repeated over and over that it is a "one-way street," and that is not a metaphor, because proxidine's effect on the user is to make the trajectory literally infinite. There is no point searching for the "mother" outside ecstasy for she is within it, implicitly, and all along the path of drug use she changes, taking on every conceivable form, in an incoherent and irresponsible succession, which leads the user astray as dreams abuse the sleeping mind."

JULY 29, 1998